A Walk on the Wylder Side

by

Laura Strickland

The Wylder West

This is a work of fiction. Names, characters, places, and incidents are either the product of the author's imagination or are used fictitiously, and any resemblance to actual persons living or dead, business establishments, events, or locales, is entirely coincidental.

A Walk on the Wylder Side

Contact Information: info@thewildrosepress.com

Cover Art by *Tina Lynn Stout*

The Wild Rose Press, Inc.
PO Box 708
Adams Basin, NY 14410-0708
Visit us at www.thewildrosepress.com

Publishing History
First Cactus Rose Edition, 2020
Trade Paperback ISBN 978-1-5092-3425-7
Digital ISBN 978-1-5092-3426-4

The Wylder West
Published in the United States of America

He wore a gun. No, two of them, one on either hip.

Cissy still hadn't got used to that. People in Chicago owned guns, sure. And unsavory elements there went about performing even more unsavory deeds, with the help of those firearms. But they didn't strut around with pistols strapped to their sides the way men—and some women—did in Wylder, Wyoming.

This man wore his weapons low, like some sort of gunslinger, and looked more than prepared to use them. Or maybe he just sought to shield them from the deluge of water.

Apart from that, he wasn't one of Mrs. Culpepper's roomers, all of whom Cissy recognized. He looked about thirty, a tall man, and lean with it—those hips certainly were lean—with a well-sculpted face now expressing extreme shock. He wore black—black trousers with a black shirt and leather vest. His hair was also black, longish in the back, and at the moment sodden.

For an instant frozen in time, Cissy stared at him and he stared back at her as if nothing—no one—else existed.

Praise for Laura Strickland

"The setting is vivid. The characters are three dimensional. The plot takes so many turns…this story will have you biting your nails to the last page."

~Sandra Dailey, Author

~*~

"Laura Strickland is an excellent writer. She really brings the setting and the characters alive, and I'd like to read more.... Laura Strickland is an author to watch."

~Marilyn Baron, Author

~*~

"The historical detail and storyline meshed well. The characters resonated with me, and I felt what they felt. This one definitely goes in the 'will read again' pile."

~Cocktails and Books Review

Chapter One

Wylder, Wyoming Territory, June 1878

"What is the meaning of this? Get up, you lazy girl, and on your feet. Back to work! What did I tell you about slacking off in the middle of a task?"

The harsh words came accompanied by a slap to the shoulder that roused Cissy Arkwright from the first good sleep she'd had in weeks. She jerked her chin up from her chest, and her eyelids flew open on a wave of alarm.

That voice—again. It seemed all she'd heard since arriving here in the town of Wylder, Wyoming, and taking up a menial position at Culpepper's Boarding House. It chased her through her days like the squawk of an angry jay, and haunted what little rest she managed to snatch at night.

Sure enough, when her weary eyes focused, she beheld her new employer, Eulalia Culpepper, standing over her, gaze narrowed in rage and face almost as crimson as her tightly wound bun of red hair.

Six days Cissy had been here in Wylder. Or was it seven? Heaven help her, she'd lost count. The time since her arrival had blurred into a haze of scrubbing and mopping, of peeling vegetables and hanging endless loads of laundry out in the dusty yard. But yes, she'd come in on the train last Saturday. Yesterday had been Friday. She'd been here a week.

"Well, Cecilia?" Mrs. Culpepper screeched at her. "I expect better than to find you *asleep* when you should be working. What do you have to say for yourself?"

Oh, Cissy could think of plenty to say. A thousand words rushed through her head, and in days not long past she would probably have spit them all out. Precious little biting of the tongue ever, for Cecilia Arkwright. But getting banished from her home with Aunt Amelia and Uncle Benjamin, back in Chicago, had taught her a few hard lessons. So she caught hold of her all-too-ready temper and sought desperately for a measure of courtesy.

Mrs. Culpepper liked courtesy in an employee. Actually, she liked humility even better, but Cissy didn't think she could manage that.

"I apologize, Mrs. Culpepper. I just sat down for a minute after I finished scrubbing the floor and must have dozed off."

"Sat down?" Mrs. Culpepper's eyes glinted, cold as ice. "What do you mean by sitting idle in the middle of the afternoon?"

Cissy drew a deep breath. It was no longer the middle of the afternoon. Supper had been over hours ago, and outside the boarding house, dusk gathered. Cissy had been up out of her bed before dawn, performing every sort of chore Mrs. Culpepper could devise. Just when she believed the end was in sight, after she'd cleaned up from supper and washed a mountain of dishes, Mrs. Culpepper had decided the kitchen floor needed cleaning.

"Better to get it done before you go to bed," she'd

told Cissy. "You'll thank me in the morning."

Cissy had performed the chore, which involved hefting a large kettle of water onto and off of the monster of a stove. She'd crawled all over that plank floor with her knees and back aching, longing for her bed all the while. The bucket of water and the mop still stood beside the back door.

When she'd finished, Cissy sat down on a chair so she wouldn't walk on that floor and mark it all up again. And she'd slipped into a dream…one of escape from this place, and a tall, dark knight who offered rescue.

Now she got to her feet. "I just thought I'd better stay in one place while the floor dried."

"A likely story." Mrs. Culpepper hiked up her chin and stared down her nose at Cissy. "You haven't even done a good job with the floor."

Anger stirred in Cissy's breast. "I have so done a good job." Despite her exhaustion—and let it be admitted, her resentment—she always put her best effort into what she did. She'd scrubbed those boards within an inch of their lives and even got the grime out of the corners.

"You have not. I should make you do it all over again."

The rage simmering in Cissy's chest rose in a bright bubble to her head.

Do not let go of that bubble, she ordered herself. Look where your hasty tongue has got you so far.

Booted clean out of her home back in Chicago, that was where, and away from her young brother, Andrew, whom she'd been forced to abandon to Aunt Amelia's dubious mercy. Not that her life with Aunt Amelia and

Uncle Benjamin had been easy, living on charity, so to speak, her presence in addition to Andy's barely tolerated.

Even though Uncle Benjamin was her blood relation—her father's brother—it had been Aunt Amelia who made the decision to send Cissy west. *I have a good friend in Wylder, Wyoming. She runs a boarding house there and is always in need of help. Maybe she'll be able to straighten the girl out.*

After no more than a week, Cissy knew why Eulalia Culpepper was in constant need of help. No one stayed working for her. Nobody in her right mind would.

But Cissy had little choice. Aunt Amelia had agreed to keep Andy with her in Chicago, and enrolled at school, if Cissy moved out. In fact, half of the pay Cissy earned working here would be sent back to Chicago for Andy's keep. Not that Aunt Amelia and Uncle Benjamin needed it. A matter of principle, Aunt Amelia said.

Cissy could think of only one thing worse than life alone here in Wylder, and that was uprooting Andy and asking him to suffer along with her. She needed time to plan a life for them, somewhere else—somewhere civilized. So she held on, somehow, to the bubble of anger.

"That would be very wasteful, Mrs. Culpepper."

"Wasteful?"

"I'd hate to squander the firewood required to strike up the stove again, to say nothing of my time."

Mrs. Culpepper's eyes narrowed. "That's what you're worried about, is it? Your time. I suppose you want to be away to your bed."

She did, she sincerely did. Weariness ravaged her senses and ate at her spirit. The last decent sleep she'd enjoyed came the night before Aunt Amelia, with a smug look on her face, had informed her of the plans to send her west. Oh, she'd dozed on the train out from Chicago, but since arriving here, tired as she was, she could catch no real rest, and started worrying the moment her head hit her lumpy pillow.

Was Aunt Amelia being kind to Andy, with Cissy gone? Andy, only eight years old, needed plenty of kindness. Ma and Pa's deaths nearly a year ago, in a train derailment, had destroyed his world. He required stability, and right now that meant staying in Chicago.

Just till Cissy could get on her feet and get him the heck out of Aunt Amelia's house for good.

Mrs. Culpepper propped her fists on her hips. "Amelia told me in her letters that you were difficult. Lippy, she called you, always with the back talk. And reckless. Turned down no fewer than three suitors, did you?"

"Two," Cissy corrected. "they were—"

"Nobody good enough for you, she said. Ideas above yourself. Send her to me, I told her. Keep the boy but send the worrisome girl to me. I'll teach her to have big ideas, and start her at the bottom. Well, girl, this kitchen floor's the bottom, and you will learn. So get to work and scrub it all over again."

Cissy shot to her feet so quickly she knocked the chair over, and glared at her employer.

"You don't need a housemaid. You need a slave."

An unpleasant smile crossed Mrs. Culpepper's face. "Wrong. I already have one, and her name's Cecilia Arkwright. Now, what do you have to say about it?"

Even amid her rage, Cissy grasped that Mrs. Culpepper was baiting her. She shouldn't, she couldn't rise to that bait. If she did, things would only get worse.

"You are a despicable woman." Had she said that out loud? She hadn't intended to. But the anger in Mrs. Culpepper's eyes increased, and her voice once more raised to a screech.

"And you, my girl, are every bit as defiant as my dear friend Amelia said. No wonder she no longer wanted you in her home. Now, empty out that bucket of water, get down on your knees, and wash this floor again."

For an instant longer Cissy stood, wrangling her anger, and trembling with the effort. She wanted to pick up the bucket and throw the dirty water in Mrs. Culpepper's face, watch it seep through her tight helmet of scraped-back hair and trickle in brown rivulets down her beet-red face. But, despite what this woman said about her, she was far too well bred—surely—to put on such a display of bad manners.

Instead, without a word, she snatched up the bucket, flung open the kitchen door and, putting all her anger into it, tossed the dirty water out into the yard.

"What in holy hell!"

The protestation had a soggy sound, probably because it came from the man who, standing in the gloom just outside the back door, had received the brunt of the water. Cissy, the bucket still raised between her hands, blinked at him in astonishment. Nobody should be in the yard, not at this time of night. And anyway, she didn't know this fellow, did she?

Hard to tell, seeing as how the water had hit him in

the upper chest and splashed right into his face. And hair. He sputtered and did a little dance before reaching for his gun belt.

He wore a gun. No, two of them, one on either hip.

Cissy still hadn't got used to that. People in Chicago owned guns, sure. And unsavory elements there went about performing even more unsavory deeds, with the help of those firearms. But they didn't strut around with pistols strapped to their sides the way men—and some women—did in Wylder, Wyoming.

This man wore his weapons low, like some sort of gunslinger, and looked more than prepared to use them. Or maybe he just sought to shield them from the deluge of water.

Apart from that, he wasn't one of Mrs. Culpepper's roomers, all of whom Cissy recognized. He looked about thirty, a tall man, and lean with it—those hips certainly were lean—with a well-sculpted face now expressing extreme shock. He wore black—black trousers with a black shirt and leather vest. His hair was also black, longish in the back, and at the moment sodden.

For an instant frozen in time, Cissy stared at him and he stared back at her as if nothing—no one—else existed.

Behind Cissy, Mrs. Culpepper howled. "Stupid girl! What have you done?" She seized Cissy by the arm and hauled her backward into the kitchen.

"What's he doing there?" Cissy lowered the now-empty bucket to her side.

Mrs. Culpepper spoke in a rush, "Mister, I'm sorry. The girl's a nuisance and a caution. You can see what I put up with, dealing with the help. If I might ask, though, what are you doing out in my yard?"

He sputtered. A trickle of dirty water ran from his lips. "I'm looking for a room. Mr. Mountroy, over at the bank, sent me. I knocked at the front but nobody answered, and since I heard voices back here—"

What he meant was, he'd heard shouting, the sound of Mrs. Culpepper scolding Cissy. Cissy set down the bucket and scowled, even as Mrs. Culpepper barked at her, "Get a cloth. Help Mister—Mister, er—"

"Saunders."

"—help Mr. Saunders dry off."

Mr. Saunders stepped into the kitchen and shut the door behind him. Little trickles of brown water dripped from his clothing onto Cissy's nice clean floor.

Damn it all. Yes, she knew she shouldn't swear, even in her head. But—dang!

She snatched up the cloth she'd used to dry the vegetables for supper and handed it to him. He swabbed his face, swiped at his chest, and carefully took the pistols from their holsters and laid them on the kitchen table.

"Are you Mrs. Culpepper?"

"I am Eulalia Culpepper, yes."

"Do you have a room? Mr. Mountroy's hired me for security at the bank. I don't have a place to stay. The other boarding house farther down the street is full. So I'm hoping you have space."

Security, eh? That probably explained the pistols. He was a guard. Shouldn't he be guarding the bank at night?

"Mr. Mountroy's a fine man, and a personal friend of mine. Unfortunately, the only room I have available right now is here, off the kitchen, alongside the help."

Mrs. Culpepper made a disdainful gesture toward Cissy.

Mr. Saunders eyed Cissy slowly, from her shoes upward. His gaze—every bit as black as his hair and clothing—lingered on the front of her skirt, all damp from crawling around on the floor, and again on her hair, half escaped from its formerly neat coronet.

Aunt Amelia always decried her hair—the hair of a harridan, she called it. Though Cissy certainly couldn't help the color, could she? Tow-headed they called it; she and Andy both had hair so blonde it looked white.

No expression showed in Mr. Saunders' dark eyes, but when he finished his inspection, he raised a brow and looked at Mrs. Culpepper.

"I won't have to share a room with her, will I?"

Chapter Two

Tired as she was, Cissy expected to fall asleep the minute her head hit the pillow that night. Instead, no sooner had she donned her nightgown and crawled into bed than her eyes popped wide open and her mind began to spin.

Why, oh, why couldn't she shut off her thoughts? The same thing happened every night. No wonder she felt like she'd been dragged behind a buckboard all the way from Cheyenne.

Of course, it didn't help having a stranger in the room right next door. A stranger who wore twin pistols.

She could hear Mr. Saunders moving around, the shuffle of his feet and a cough now and again. This addition off the back of the kitchen, consisting of two small rooms for the help, had been thrown up hastily, and the partition wall was thin.

From what she'd seen, Wylder, Wyoming was a mix of hastily and well-built structures. Some, like the bank, had a certain permanency about them. Others looked like they'd blow over in the next strong wind.

Nothing like Chicago. In fact, here in the Wild West, Cissy's life had become darned near unrecognizable.

Once, she'd been the daughter of a successful real estate investor, living in reasonable luxury. After the train derailment that cost her parents their lives, Uncle

Benjamin took over their estate, and she and Andy became his dependents. Uncle Benjamin and Aunt Amelia had done their best to solve what Aunt Amelia called the "complication" of Cissy by introducing her to a series of suitors. It was her duty, so Aunt Amelia claimed, to marry and leave the bulk of the estate to Andy. Uncle Benjamin would oversee Andy's inheritance until he came of age.

When Cissy's behavior became what Aunt Amelia deemed difficult—when she approached her father's solicitor wanting to know the exact terms of his will—her aunt and uncle denounced her.

She supposed, to be fair, she *was* difficult. She rarely did as she was told, asked impertinent questions, and did her best to stand up for both herself and her young brother.

Lying in the dark, tiny room in Wylder, Wyoming, she squeezed her eyes tight shut. She missed Andy so much she ached. Was he all right? Uncle Benjamin's home wasn't exactly what she'd call a nurturing environment.

Better than Culpepper's boarding house, though. Here, she'd turned into nothing more than a drudge, who scrubbed from morning to night, and who tossed filthy water on strangers.

Next door, Mr. Saunders dropped something with a clatter. She very clearly heard him swear.

Ah, an interesting word, that one. A word Cissy quite likely shouldn't repeat. But—strangely satisfying.

The bed springs next door creaked, and she heard Mr. Saunders sigh. She pictured again the look of consternation on his face as he stood in the doorway, dripping. An interesting face, as interesting as that word he'd just uttered. Shuttered and dangerous—but handsome enough, oh, yes. A face into which Cissy wouldn't mind gazing for a considerable length of time.

But she would have to do her best to avoid Mr. Saunders. Having drenched him with water, she would not be his favorite person. And she also needed to remember if she could hear what he did in his room, he could hear her too.

As if to emphasize the point, she heard his bed frame creak as he rolled over. The sound, so near at hand, proved somehow comforting. Mr. Saunders was a guard, after all. He and his pistols were right next door.

Oddly reassured, she closed her eyes and slid away into sleep.

****

Buck Standish—also known as Burt Saunders—checked his pistols one more time before sliding them into their holsters. A compulsion of his, something upon which his life had ridden for far too long.

As he slid the weapons into place, his thumbs rubbed over the initials carved into the grips. *B. S.* Folks here in Wylder, where he played a part other than his own, might think the *S* stood for Saunders. In truth it stood for Standish instead. For that was his true name: Buckminster—or Buck—Standish, a moniker of considerable renown.

Could a man outrun his past? Could Buck Standish? He sincerely doubted it. Nothing but trouble had ever followed him, and he'd learned to expect little other than bad luck. Yet if ever there was a town where a man might lose himself, it would have to be one like Wylder, here in the wide-open Wyoming Territory.

It would take only one person recognizing him to

scuttle his chances of turning honest and putting the gunslinging life behind him. Ironic—at one time he'd cherished his dangerous reputation. Yet the guns coming after him seemed to get younger and younger. He wanted no part of facing off against mere boys.

But sure as anything, if his true name got out, some damn fool would show up wanting to take him down. One always did.

With a last caress for the pistols, he set his hat on his head. Should Mr. Mountroy find out who he was, Buck didn't know if he'd keep him in the job of bank guard. He'd probably think that tantamount to letting the fox keep watch over the chicken coop. And really, what else was he fit for? He'd been earning his way with his guns since shortly after he left home at fourteen. He'd hired out to some of the most notorious and unprincipled men in the West.

Was Mountroy one of those? If he did discover the security he'd hired—one Burt Saunders—was actually the hired gun Buckminster Standish, would that be an end to it? Was Mountroy an ethical man?

Buck's gut told him no. And when it came to weighing men, his gut was rarely wrong.

Quietly, because his movements were always careful, he opened the door of his room. A woman stood in the kitchen with her back to him. She wore a brown dress with a white apron tied over it, and her hair hung down her back in a long braid, so blonde it looked white.

Jesus, it was the woman who'd thrown the water all over him last evening.

The water had been lukewarm and dirty, and smelled of lye soap. Not an experience he wanted to repeat soon. He'd better be sure to keep from startling her, because now she had a cast iron frying pan in her hand.

"Good morning."

She spun around and gaped at him. Not doing a very good job of keeping from spooking her, was he? As they had last night after she drenched him, they spent several seconds staring at each other.

She might be a clumsy housemaid, but nobody could say she wasn't striking to look at. Not pretty, as such, but the sort to gather and hold a man's notice. In fact, looking at her, the word *pretty* fairly faded to insignificance. She had pale skin, now being overtaken by a rosy flush, and a pair of expressive blue eyes, the color of the sky over the prairie. She also had a stubborn mouth, and a chin with a good deal of strength to it. And that hair—oh, sweet lord, that hair!

He wondered how she'd ended up here, instead of safely tucked away as somebody's wife. Scrubbing floors in a second-class boarding house like this.

"Morning," she returned a bit breathlessly. She worked at the sink, which was piled high with a veritable mountain of dirty dishes, including that frying pan.

"Where's the dining room?" he asked. Mrs. Culpepper hadn't showed him round the place last night, just the bit of a room he'd hired.

Her eyes widened. "Did you want breakfast? Oh, I'm sorry. You've missed it."

"I beg your pardon?" Buck frowned. "It's plumb early."

"I know. Mrs. Culpepper cuts off breakfast service at seven in the morning. She wants everybody up and out of their rooms so they can be cleaned."

Buck's frown turned to something darker. His stomach was so empty the front of it had stuck to his backbone. He couldn't remember the last time he'd had a decent meal. Yesterday? The day before? He'd pushed to ride on through from Laramie and been more concerned with seeing to his horse's needs last night than his own.

"Well, she might have mentioned that to me last evening."

The young woman shot a look at the door that presumably led to the rest of the house. "Mrs. Culpepper's gone out. And I've just cleared the table. You sit down here, and I'll get you something to eat."

"You sure? I wouldn't want you to get in trouble."

"It's the least I owe you, after—after last night." Her gaze moved over him and fastened on his pistols. "I hope your—er—guns didn't suffer any harm."

Before Buck could come up with an answer to that, she began clearing plates from the table and stacking them on the drainboard.

"You have to wash all those?" Buck asked.

"Oh, yes. I'm just waiting for the water to heat. Please, sit down."

He slid into a chair even as she turned away and began loading a clean plate with food from a couple of platters.

"So," he inquired, "what sin did you commit?"

She looked round in surprise. "I beg your pardon?"

"What did you do to get condemned to this purgatory?"

A smile stole across her face. It didn't come all at once—she fought it, not wanting to get too friendly with a boarder, no doubt. But it conquered her discipline and lit her face like a ray of sunshine. A dimple appeared in either cheek.

By God, a man would trade a lot to make her smile like that. Or to kiss those dimples.

She placed the loaded plate in front of him. The aroma of bacon made his nose twitch. "My sins are too many and too diverse to recount."

"Are they?" He lifted a brow. What could this young woman, with a face like a flower, know about evil deeds? Had she ever traded her conscience for money? Ever gunned a man down?

"Go ahead and eat before Mrs. Culpepper gets back. She won't like finding you here."

Buck required no more encouragement. The eggs were on the cold side and the toast burnt, but the fried potatoes and bacon were first class. He ate ravenously.

As he did, she busied herself at the sink, scraping plates and starting to wash, her back to him. It gave him a chance to admire the braid that hung down past her waist.

Only imagine all that hair loose, reaching all the way down to her firm little butt.

"So you didn't say," he spoke as he swabbed his plate with the last of the toast. "How did you end up here in Wylder?"

She turned around and dried her hands on her apron. "My family, back in Chicago, wanted shed of me. Take warning, Mr. Saunders. I'm a woman who's been labeled *difficult*."

It was his turn to smile. "Don't scare me none, Miss. I've been known to wear that label myself."

Chapter Three

He'd forgotten to ask her name. Buck thought of that as soon as he set out walking for the bank down on Wylder Street. Goldmount Bank it was called, no doubt in honor of owner and proprietor Frederick Mountroy.

Sure was pretty country, Buck acknowledged as he went. And he'd seen a lot of scenery, from Montana right through to California, mostly from the back of a horse.

Seldom enough did he have his boots on the ground.

Beautiful as it was here, though, it couldn't compare with what he'd seen back in the kitchen at Mrs. Culpepper's boarding house. That thought surprised him. He was no poet. And he usually went for a different sort of woman altogether, one willing to entertain a fellow for a night or two, no strings attached, when the need proved great. Not some well-bred innocent from the east.

Difficult, she said. Ha, well, as he'd told her, he had a personal acquaintance with that.

The bank came into view, perched in the middle of the block like a queen amidst a huddle of peasants. A fine structure, indeed, Mr. Mountroy had built, made of wood, sure, but two stories high, with a handsome façade that included a plank porch with tall pillars. The other fellow Mountroy employed as a guard stood out front, his pistol very much in evidence.

From what Mountroy had told Buck's old companion and mentor, Pete, who'd sent Buck down here to take the position, Mountroy didn't think much of his current guard. The bank had been held up twice with the man on duty. Besides, this was a two-man job, and should be taken in shifts.

Fred Mountroy was an old acquaintance of Pete's—something that gave Buck pause in and of itself. Anybody with Pete for a friend couldn't be completely above board. Buck should know.

"You go on down there and take this job," Pete had urged Buck. "That bank has got a reputation as a soft target. You're just what Fred Mountroy needs." He stared at Buck with his queer-colored eyes, one green and one brown. "And the job's just what you need, if you want to get out of the life."

The life of a gun for hire, that was.

"But," Buck had objected, "if I'm recognized—"

"Use a new name. Wylder's out of the way. You might get lucky."

He might. Then again, lady luck had never smiled on him much. It sure hadn't been lucky being born Oliver Standish's son, or having his ma die giving birth to her third child, a little girl, when he was only eight. The child had also died, leaving Buck and his sister, Abbigail, to be raised by their sadistic drunk of a father. He blinked rapidly at the sudden rush of memories. He'd tried his best to protect Abbigail, while growing up. In the end, he'd had to get away.

His lips twisted in a wry smile. Maybe he could attribute his quick reflexes to luck, but he suspected they came of learning early to dodge his father's fist.

He paused on the board sidewalk in front of the bank. The guard eyed him, starting with his dusty black boots and taking a bit of time over the twin pistols.

"Morning," Buck said.

"Morning," the fellow returned, not very happily.

"Mr. Mountroy in?"

"Not yet. Should be here any minute, though."

Buck pasted an affable smile on his face and stuck out his hand. "I'm Burt Saunders. Mr. Mountroy hired me for security here."

The fellow's face brightened. "Lloyd Winters." He shook Buck's hand heartily. "Glad to see you." Winters was perhaps thirty-five, with a rough-at-the-edges appearance and a worried expression. "Thought for a minute you'd come to rob the place, with them fancy pistols."

They weren't fancy particularly, but they sure were accurate.

Buck quirked an eyebrow. "In broad daylight?"

"Been held up twice in daylight. Robbers rode in bold as brass and bulled their way in. Second time, shots were fired. I got nicked in the arm." Winters rocked on his heels. "Third time, I stood 'em off till the sheriff got here."

"Third time?" Pete hadn't mentioned that.

"Here comes Mr. Mountroy now." Winters gestured up the street. Buck turned and narrowed his eyes.

Fred Mountroy was a big man with bulky shoulders, clad in a suit of fine black broadcloth. Maybe forty years old, he was losing his hair and had a pair of the shrewdest eyes Buck had ever encountered.

Like the guard, he eyed Buck up and down. A

smile of satisfaction quirked his mustached mouth. They'd met last night, if only briefly, when Buck rode in. "Morning, Mr. Saunders."

"Mr. Mountroy." Buck stuck out his hand again. Mountroy's clasp felt firm and dry.

Mountroy fished a key from his vest pocket and unlocked the front door of the bank. "Come on in. Lloyd, you can go home now. See you again this evening."

Lloyd's face creased. "Nights? I still gotta work nights? But I thought as senior guard—"

Mountroy clasped Winters' shoulder. "Just for now. We'll talk about a schedule after Burt, here, settles in. Right?"

Lloyd went off, and Mountroy swept Buck inside.

The interior of the bank smelled like money. It wasn't a scent Buck could describe, but it was there. An open area led to a railing with a gate, with a row of tellers' windows beyond. Past that stood a couple of desks and a door set in a paneled wall.

"So," Mr. Mountroy said, leading the way through the gate, "you're Pete Beckstall's protégé?"

"Protégé?" Buck repeated.

"It means—"

"I know what it means, Mr. Mountroy." He wasn't ignorant. "Just not sure the term fits."

Mountroy paused and gave him a long look. "Son, let's get this straight from the get-go. I know exactly who and what you are."

Alarm raced through Buck. He disguised it and raised a brow. "What am I, Mr. Mountroy?"

"You really want me to say it out plain? No matter, you're what I need. I can't sustain any more big losses.

Better to keep you in my pay than have the vault emptied out again."

Keep you in my pay. Buck had been kept in men's pay before, and done some terrible things at their bidding, the sort of things that would probably, one day, send him straight to Hell. If he believed in that particular place.

Mountroy pushed through the door behind the tellers' windows. "This here is my office. And that's the vault. Sit yourself down. Want a drink?"

"It's barely eight in the morning."

"I know."

Buck cooled a bit. "No, thanks." His father used to start drinking early in the morning. Some days he never quit. "Mr. Mountroy, I have a couple concerns."

"The position?"

"The position's fine."

"Pete says you're looking for a new start." Mr. Mountroy pulled a flask from a drawer in his desk. "Want to put the old ways behind you."

Ah, so Pete had told him that. "I do. I've had it up to here," Buck indicated his ear, "with gunning men down."

"I hope not. I will expect you to shoot anyone who tries to rob this place again. I'm not fooling."

"Yeah." Well, he didn't have to shoot to kill.

"Anyway, son, a man's got to make a living, right? Even after he hangs up his guns. Which means you can't—hang up your guns, I mean. Not quite yet."

"That's not what concerns me so much as the possibility of getting recognized."

Mountroy gave him a bland stare. "You're Burt Saunders, are you not?"

"You know what I mean. Men tend to track me down. To challenge me. They want to find out if they're faster. That happens, it won't be good for me or you."

"You think I'm afraid to let folks know I've hired a gunslinger? You don't know me. Or Wylder. Don't worry, Burt. We're out of the way—at least, we were till the railroad came through. And nobody's going to expect the great Buckminster Standish to be standing guard at a bank in Wylder, Wyoming."

"It's your funeral, Mr. Mountroy, if it all comes undone."

"I'll take my chances. Now, Mr. Saunders, since Lloyd's gone home, why don't you start work? Take your place out front, and let folks see them pretty pistols."

"Sure thing, Mr. Mountroy." Buck got up. He'd let folks see his sidearms—so long as nobody got too close a look at them.

Chapter Four

The new boarder never returned to Mrs. Culpepper's till after six o'clock that evening. By then, he was nearly late for supper.

"Mr. Saunders," Mrs. Culpepper scolded him as he took the last available seat at the table, "I run a punctual house, as I'm sure my other boarders will attest." She waved a hand at the other three men in attendance, all of whom had rooms upstairs. Mr. Petrie ran the post office, and lived here permanently. The other two were transients, and nothing to brag about, if anyone asked Cissy's opinion.

Which nobody did.

"Mrs. Culpepper," Sanders replied politely, "my shift at the bank runs till six o'clock. Not much I can do about it. And, the way I understand it, supper's included in my board."

"And my servant," Mrs. Culpepper put her nose in the air, "is waiting to clear the table."

Servant? Huh! Darned if she was. Cissy wiped her hands on her apron and spoke up. "That's all right, Mrs. Culpepper. Let him eat. I don't mind, and I have other chores to do."

The rest of the guests scattered. Saunders shot Cissy a grateful glance and—

Had he just winked at her? Had he?

She picked up two of the empty plates and pushed

through into the kitchen. Mrs. Culpepper swept in after her.

"Cecilia, do not coddle the guests. I've been keeping rooming houses in one city or another for a long time. Believe me when I say men like that will take every advantage."

Men like that?

"Best to lay the ground rules at the outset. Otherwise we'll be serving him supper at all hours of the night."

Perfectly aware that sound—and their conversation—traveled through the door to the dining room, Cissy said, "I just thought since his board does, in fact, include two meals a day—"

"He forfeits the privilege if he isn't on time. Now, get this kitchen cleaned up, and do it right."

She sailed back out. Cissy scraped down the plates—not much left on them—before stepping into the dining room for a second load.

Saunders sat there in splendid isolation like a king at his banquet table. He'd taken what was left on the platters and ate with apparent enjoyment, though he paused with his knife and fork aloft when she came in.

The eyebrow went up. "Cecilia?"

"I beg your pardon?"

"That's your name?"

Cissy flushed. She wasn't sure why.

"Cecilia Arkwright." She extended a hand across the table. "Pleased to make your acquaintance."

"Bu—Burt Saunders. The same." His fingers felt warm and rough. She half expected to experience a tingle or something, having an attractive man holding onto her hand that way.

"Thanks for taking my part, Miss Cecilia—again. I don't want to cause you any trouble." He smiled, a slow thing that spread across his face and put light in his black eyes. Ah, there came the tingle. Lord, have mercy.

"I'm usually in trouble." She took back her fingers and cocked one hip. "Goes with the territory."

"I've just met my erstwhile hostess, and already I don't see how you can stand working for the woman."

"Needs must. I have a little brother back east. Me being here is—well, part of the conditions for keeping him where he's comfortable."

"Back east, where?"

"Chicago."

"Wylder, Wyoming's a far cry from Chicago." Was that curiosity Cissy saw in his eyes?

"That it is."

"Sure would like to hear the rest of your story sometime."

"It's not as interesting as you'd think." Cissy picked up two more plates and carried them out. When she returned for the cups, he said, "Sorry to hold you up."

"Please, don't worry about it. These dishes will take me an hour anyway." She leaned toward him. "Tell you what. If you get detained at the bank and arrive too late in the future, I'll hold a plate for you. Just come to the kitchen, and you can have it there."

His gaze clung to hers. "Don't want to be a bother."

"Won't be. I usually eat supper after, anyhow. We could—could eat together."

"That sounds real fine."

“And—if you want to come into the kitchen when you’re finished here, I saved a piece of cake you can have for dessert.” She needn’t tell him she’d saved that piece for herself.

“I’ll take you up on that, Miss Cecilia. And thank you for your kindness.”

Now, what had made her invite him to have supper with her? Cissy wondered as she returned to the kitchen.

Miss Cecilia. She liked the sound of that.

He came in quietly only a short time later, carrying his own plate. She had her hands in the soapy water by then, but dried them off and fetched his slice of cake. He made himself comfortable at the kitchen table and dug in.

“You make this cake, Miss Cecilia?”

“Yes, Mr. Saunders, I did.”

“Sure is good. In fact I think this may well be the best cake I ever tasted. You’re a woman of many talents.”

“My aunt in Chicago, with whom I lived—where my brother, Andy is now—might disagree with you. But my mother was a fancy baker. In fact, baking runs in her family, and she taught me well. Aunt Amelia is far more practical. She’s determined a woman should be able to prepare a full menu for the servants to follow, and organize a dinner party. She should be able to sew, as well as embroider.”

He looked up, surprised. “Servants? But—”

She faced him and propped a hand on her hip. “You thought I was a servant? Well, I imagine it seems that way. Do not be mistaken, Mr. Saunders, my presence here is a punishment doled out by my aunt.

She is not a nice woman. In fact, she's bosom friends with Mrs. Culpepper, so that will tell you something."

"Punishment." He pushed away his empty plate and made a face. "Seems to me, in this life half the time the wrong folks end up getting punished."

"Far too often, in my opinion."

He got to his feet, towering over her. With his dark eyes fixed on hers, he suddenly seemed too large—too male—for the kitchen. "Yeah, Miss Cecilia, and sometimes it seems somebody ought to make that right."

****

A week went by, in the slow crawl that now passed for Cissy's life. She plowed her way through the endless chores to which she was assigned, dodged Mrs. Culpepper's ill temper, and wrote to Andy, back home.

Mr. Saunders rarely made it to the boarding house in time for supper. Instead of facing the irascible landlady, he took to coming around back to the kitchen, where Cissy had his supper put aside, keeping warm. The first few times, he ate at the big kitchen table while she washed dishes. After that she began holding her supper also, and sitting down with him to have the meal. Seated across from each other, they would talk of this or that—nothing weighty or serious. But it came to be those times, or the promise of them, that got Cissy through her days.

She found a certain comfort in sharing the meal and conversation with him, dividing the last piece of pie, watching the light come and go in his dark eyes when he spoke. She liked his sense of humor, dry and wicked—it complemented her own all too well. She looked forward to his rare smile and—she supposed she just found his presence enjoyable.

She also found comfort in hearing him move around in his room next to her own, at night. She slept better knowing he was there, better than at any time since she'd come west.

Mrs. Culpepper, eager to put her feet up and devote her attention to her knitting, rarely came to the kitchen after supper. When she did put her head in the room, usually checking up on Cissy's efforts, Mr. Saunders was always in his room.

That was what Cissy called him—Mr. Saunders, all right and proper. He continued to call her Miss Cecilia, which seemed proper too.

They were acquaintances. Maybe bordering on friends. Nothing more.

Yet Cissy couldn't deny the way her heart bounded when she heard his step outside the kitchen door—for she learned that quickly—or how her spirits lifted when that door opened and he smiled at her. She got the impression Burt Saunders didn't smile often. When he did—oh, when he did, it changed everything. It felt like a gift, that smile. And knowing they could talk together, that she could unleash her sense of humor and share her thoughts with someone, made all the difference.

She started making fancier and fancier desserts, fussing over them, just so she could see that light take hold in his eyes when she produced the portion she held back for him. And for the first time since she'd come west, she began to think of Wylder as something other than a punishment. The days might be hard, but when Mr. Saunders entered her kitchen of an evening, everything came right.

Chapter Five

Buck awoke and attempted to stretch in the bed that was much too small for him. He'd slept in a lot of different places over the course of his life, some considerably more comfortable than others. Mrs. Culpepper's wasn't the worst. That would have to go to his cramped berth in the upstairs room of his father's house, where he'd too often lain listening while Pa drank downstairs, spewing a drunkard's words, getting wilder and wilder till he'd climb the stairs with a strap in his hand.

And Mrs. Culpepper's—well, it did have its compensations. Like the best pie he'd ever tasted. And, quite possibly, some of the best company.

Last night, though, had been a rough one. The old memories had gone walking through his mind the way they sometimes did, far sharper than any nightmare.

A funny thing, the human mind. It held on to so many things from long ago, and far too clearly. Like the faces of the men with whom he'd squared off over the years—Jesus, if he had to describe them in daylight, he didn't suppose he could, but when he closed his eyes to sleep, they came walking up in front of him again. He saw the emotions in their faces once more. Bold, daring—excited. Some doubtful at the last instant, when they went for their guns.

Lately, they'd been getting younger and younger.

Some of them looked downright green. Worse, some of them reminded Buck of himself, back in the days when he'd left home. After he met Pete, and learned not just to use a gun but to draw it with skill.

Had it been a touch of good luck, after all, that had kept him alive then? Maybe. But eventually every man's luck ran out. Would this town, Wylder, Wyoming, be the place where that happened to him?

He rose, the ropes on the bed creaking, washed himself in the basin, and dressed quickly. His thoughts moved again to the young woman next door. Would she already be up and at work, tackling one of her endless chores? Maybe if he left now, before breakfast, he could avoid seeing her. For one thing he knew for sure—Miss Cecilia Arkwright deserved better company than him.

Sure enough, the kitchen lay empty when he stepped out. He went swiftly through the door and into the morning. When he reached the street, he narrowed his eyes. Quiet at this hour, it certainly wouldn't be later on. Most of the shops were still closed. The folks who'd kicked up their heels last night—the drifters, ranch hands in from their spreads, mountain men down from their trapping lines, gamblers and their hired lady friends—still slept.

In front of the bank, Lloyd Winters remained on duty, sitting in the chair placed there, tipped back on its rear legs. Buck wondered whether the fellow dozed off during the night or if, maybe, his thoughts haunted him, too.

He grimaced. Worse than seeing the faces of those he'd bested with his guns were the other, even older memories—of life at home before Ma died, when things were still good. Those tugged not only at his emotions but his heart.

The face of his sister, when they stood together at Ma's grave. They hadn't known then how things would change. And the way she'd looked when Pa started to hollering. Oliver Standish was a curious man—educated in England, and with money in his pockets, he should have led a sedate, comfortable life. But the Standish men weren't created for sedate and comfortable. Pa had wanted adventure and had dragged his wife and young son—for Buck was only three at that time—westward across an ocean to a new land. Not satisfied with that, he'd kept moving, breaking his wife's health in the process. Abby had been born in this raw, new land. Disregarding Ma's weakened constitution, Pa had foisted another child on her, the daughter that had ended her life.

Oliver Standish had always liked to drink, but after that he took to whisky like a fish to water. A devil rode the man, and he'd turned mean.

Buck angled down Sidewinder Lane in an effort to avoid Lloyd, not in the mood for conversation. No, not even with the delightfully tart-tongued Miss Cecilia. Anyway, if he hung around the boarding house, he'd just hear Mrs. Culpepper begin hollering at her. He couldn't abide the sound of raised voices. And if Mrs. Culpepper kept it up, Buck might just give her a dressing down he'd enjoy—and that would likely get him tossed out on his ear.

A vision of Cecilia rose before his mind's eye, so real she might be standing in front of him. That hair, like spun white gold, and the defiant tilt to her chin. The spark of something rebellious and unmanageable in her blue eyes that hinted at intelligence and humor and maybe—just maybe—passion. She had a sprinkling of freckles across her nose, and the sweetest pair of breasts he'd ever seen.

If this town—Wylder—could truly give him an opportunity to start over, he'd want a chance with a woman like that.

Don't be a fool. You already know you're not worthy of a woman like that. Sure, he had some money tucked away, but it was blood money, earned the ugly way. The only other thing he had to offer Miss Cecilia was a false name and a dangerous reputation.

The sun, streaming in from the east, nearly blinded him as he emerged onto Old Cheyenne Road. On his left lay the railroad tracks and, farther off, the Wylder County Social Club—all shuttered tight at this hour.

Down along on the left, he spied the livery and decided to stop in and see Midnight. Lately, apart from Pete, the horse had been his only friend. He wanted to make sure the fellow at the livery was looking after him right.

He found Chet Daniels on the job early. Buck could see him leading horses out into the corral before mucking out the stalls.

Midnight was still in his box. He whickered and tossed his black head when he saw Buck, asking for an apple. Buck went to him and ran a gentle hand down his nose. One thing he'd learned from watching Pa—a man, a real man that was, should be gentle with those he cared about.

"Sorry, fella, I didn't bring you anything. Didn't know I was coming. You doing all right?"

Midnight blew some air and nudged Buck's

shoulder. The familiar, warm smell of horse came to Buck's nose.

He'd always got on better with horses, with animals in general, than with people. His father, who'd fancied himself a connoisseur of horseflesh, had owned some fine stock over the years. But the bastard beat his horses, the same as his son.

"Mr. Saunders, isn't it?"

Daniels stood behind him, his hat pushed to the back of his head and an inquiring expression on his face. No longer young, the man had a weathered appearance about him, and honest brown eyes.

Buck hastily sought control of himself. He rarely displayed his emotions, and weakness least of all.

"Morning," he said. "Just thought I'd swing by and visit this fellow before I start my shift at the bank."

"He's a grand animal. And you can see I'm looking after him."

Midnight's box was clean, and his hayrack nearly full.

"I sure do appreciate it. He's carried me many a mile, and deserves the rest."

"Gotta respect a man who looks after his horse. Want to lead him outside for me?"

Buck did so, the two of them walking together back out into the sunshine.

"I reckon this place is a fulltime job," Buck remarked.

Daniels snorted. "You can say that again. And I'm not as young as I used to be. The kid I hired to help me muck out took off yesterday. Said he had ambitions and they didn't include shoveling horse shit. Can you credit it?"

Buck laughed, his spirits lifting.

"Why, in my day we learned the value of hard work. I'll be here after sundown every day, at least till I find somebody else to help. What I need is a partner, someone to buy into this place, so I can start to take it easy."

Buck eyed the man, from his grayed head down to his gnarled knuckles. "Tell you what, I'm early for my shift at the bank. Why don't you let me give you a hand for an hour or so?"

Daniels looked surprised. "You sure you want to go to your job smelling like horses?"

Buck flashed a smile. "I can think of worse things to smell like. Anyway, I don't mind the company of horses."

"Nor do I. Well, I won't say no, Mr. Saunders, just this once. And I sure do appreciate it."

Buck rolled up the sleeves of his shirt. "Where's your pitchfork?"

Nearly an hour later, he used a bandana to mop the sweat from his brow and the grime from his hands. Pete always said good hard work never hurt a man. In the old days, Buck had argued it. Now he had to admit—whether it was the company of the horses or Chet Daniels' silent presence, he felt better than he had when he got out of bed.

"I'll say one thing for you, Mr. Saunders." Daniels gave him a big grin. "You ain't afraid to break your back. Or bust your balls."

"I enjoyed it." Buck went to Midnight, who stood with his head hanging over the split rail fence, and caressed his nose one last time.

"You're welcome back whenever you're astir

early," Daniels joked.

"I just might take you up on that. Look after this fella for me, will you?"

"Sure thing." Daniels eased up. "You know, if you ever get tired of Fred Mountroy's bullshit, over at the bank—"

"Bullshit?" Buck's gaze quickened.

Daniels spat with careful aim. "That man ain't the gentleman he pretends to be."

"How so?"

"Just between you and me—he's rougher round the edges than he seems. Plus, the fellow runs his business in a singular way, not like any bank I ever seen. I mean, lots of bank owners hire guards. Most those guards ain't gunslingers."

Buck stiffened. "Who said I'm a gunslinger?"

"Nobody. But I ain't anyone's fool, either." Chet's gaze dropped to Buck's pistols. "You wear them awful comfortable."

"Lots of men do. It's dangerous country. You never know when you'll have to run off undesirables—say, horse thieves."

"Good point. And no offense meant."

"None taken. I respect an honest man." Even if he couldn't claim to be one, himself.

"As I was saying, you get tired of Fred Mountroy's bullshit, I could use a partner here. A younger man, maybe one who's not afraid to work."

Buck tipped his hat. "You can be sure I'll keep your kind offer in mind."

Chapter Six

The letter arrived halfway through the morning, while Cissy busied herself baking bread. The young courier who brought it was intercepted by Mrs. Culpepper at the door, and so surrendered it to her hands.

Cissy shaped her loaves, wondering why Mr. Saunders had stepped out early that morning—so early she hadn't had a chance to catch even a glimpse of him. Mrs. Culpepper brought the message to the kitchen, her lips pursed and a pensive look pasted to her face.

"The boy said this came on the stage. For you. But it's not from your aunt."

Cissy wiped her cheek with a floury hand, which she then held out. "Please give it to me."

"I'm not at all sure I should. It doesn't say who it's from."

Cissy lifted her brows. "It doesn't matter. Mrs. Culpepper, I'm pretty certain Federal law extends out here in the Wyoming Territory. You have no right to withhold my mail."

"No need to get all huffy about it." With a sour look, Mrs. Culpepper handed over the envelope. As soon as Cissy saw the address on the front, she recognized it as Andy's painfully careful writing.

"Why, it's from my brother."

Mrs. Culpepper sniffed. "That's all right then, just

so long as it's not from some unsuitable male. There'll be none of that under my roof. And anyway, I promised your aunt I'd keep an eye on you."

"No unsuitable males." An unbidden image of Burt Saunders flashed into Cissy's head. Just as unsuitable as a man could be.

"Be sure you don't take too long reading that, away from your chores." Mrs. Culpepper stalked out. Cissy covered her loaves with a clean cloth and, leaving them to rise, sank down into a chair at the table.

An unexpected delight hearing from Andy so soon, or possibly a concern. For the letter to arrive this quick, he must have written it soon after she left Chicago.

And he wasn't fond of his pen.

Worry nibbled at her as she slit the envelope open with her thumb.

Dear Cissy,

I guess you've settled into your new place with Aunt Amelia's friend by now. Sure wish you hadn't left home. Aunt Amelia keeps saying it's for the best, that it will be good for us to be apart a while. She says you coddle me too much and I need to learn to be a man.

A man? Cissy lit with anger. The poor boy was only eight and had lost his parents less than a year ago.

I really miss you. It's not the same here with you gone. We've started our summer break at school, and Uncle Benjamin's been taking me to work with him. So I can learn the ropes.

The last three words were underlined. Cissy, torn between laughter and tears, gnawed at her lip. Had she done the right thing, leaving Andy behind? Certainly, Aunt Amelia wasn't what she'd call a nurturing woman, but surely Uncle Benjamin would keep anything bad from happening to Andy. Still frowning, she read on.

Cissy, I think there's something funny going on. Something smelly, Papa would have said. Like bad fish.

James Arkwright had been a discerning man, and he'd taught both his daughter and his son to read people and situations well.

While I was at Uncle Benjamin's office, I overheard something. Uncle Benjamin was talking with his partner, Mr. Canfield. They were talking about a will. You don't suppose they meant Papa's will, do you? Because Uncle Benjamin told us there wasn't one.

So he had. Cissy's fingers tightened on the page. She hadn't believed that—her father had been far too careful a man to neglect providing for his family in an emergency. But if he'd left a will, it would have been in the safe right there in the office the two brothers Arkwright shared.

What if—what if there had been a will after all, and it left the whole or part of the business to Cissy?

Her eyes narrowed. Not much she could do about it now, was there—not from way out here in Wyoming Territory. Nothing except write again to her father's lawyer, to whom she'd already paid visits while she was still in Chicago.

Mr. Parkinson insisted her father hadn't left a will, but he'd failed to look her in the eye while saying it. What if Mr. Parkinson was in Uncle Benjamin's pocket?

Uncle Benjamin would be in control of Father's business, that was what, at least for the next ten years or more, until Andy gained his majority.

She hated to think such things of her own uncle.

She also hated the fact that she'd left Andy at his mercy. She had to find a way—a means—to get out of this boarding house and on her feet so she could send for him.

Sure, Wylder might be the Wild West, but it couldn't be much worse than the two of them living apart.

The bottom of the letter showed smudges. Made by tears? A sympathetic sting came to Cissy's eyes as she read the end of her brother's letter.

I've written this in secret, and I'm going to mail it to you without anyone knowing. Cissy, can you fix all this? I don't like living here alone.

Could she fix all this? Sitting there at the flour-strewn table, she couldn't say how. She supposed she could return to Chicago, with or without her aunt and uncle's permission. If she turned up at their door, they'd have to take her in, right?

But she hadn't the fare, not with Mrs. Culpepper keeping part of her meager wages back, to send to Aunt Amelia for Andy's keep. Likewise, she hadn't the funds to send Andy a ticket, so he could come out to Wylder.

As if she'd allow an eight-year-old boy to travel all that way alone.

She would answer Andy's letter, try to reassure him as best she could. Maybe tell him to keep his ears open—or was that too risky?

Meanwhile, she didn't completely trust Eulalia Culpepper, Aunt Amelia's bosom friend and confidant. She often sent Cissy on errands. What was to keep the woman from searching through Cissy's belongings and reading this, while she was gone?

She folded the letter and pressed it to her lips

before she got up, nudged aside the burner cover on the stove, and fed Andy's words to the fire.

When first she'd arrived from Chicago, it had taken her days to learn how to deal with the monster of a stove. Now, they shared their duties in the dreary kitchen domain.

Let the stove keep her secrets for her. But it hurt, not having Andy's letter to keep.

Mrs. Culpepper came into the kitchen, striving to appear casual and failing miserably. Her eyes went first to the table before examining Cissy's person. Not glimpsing the letter, she glanced next at the door of Cissy's room.

"Cecilia, I would like you to go to the mercantile for me."

"I'm in the middle of baking bread, Mrs. Culpepper."

"You've set it to rise, so you'll have time, if you don't lollygag."

"I need to begin scrubbing and peeling the vegetables for supper." Mrs. Culpepper always insisted she serve a mountain of vegetables. Since they cost less than meat, she expected the boarders to fill up on them.

"I'll prepare the vegetables," she said now, with an unconvincing smile.

Cissy stared. Unprecedented! And far be it from her to miss out on taking a breather.

She dusted her hands and took off her apron. "Well, all right. What do you need?"

"A spool of white mercerized cotton. For those linens I'm mending—the ones you said you didn't have time to do. Here's a penny." Mrs. Culpepper fished deep in her pocket.

"I'll be as quick as I can, Mrs. Culpepper."

"See you do. And mind your step going down the street—stay away from those cowboys and other rough sorts."

"Yes, Mrs. Culpepper."

Cissy stepped out the back door into the sunshine and drew a deep breath. A little devil whispered in her ear, telling her if she went back inside now, she would probably catch Mrs. Culpepper in the act of poking around in her private quarters.

Of course, if she did that, she'd have to trade away her chance for a stroll down Wylder Street to the mercantile. And if she circled around and took the long way to the Post Office after, she could pass the bank where, if she was lucky, she just might catch a glimpse of Mr. Burt Saunders.

Thanks, Andy.

Chapter Seven

A frenzied pounding roused Cissy from her sleep. She'd been having pleasant dreams, for once—dreams about baking. She stood in the kitchen, not the one here in Wylder, Wyoming, but back home in Chicago. The air contained the fragrant scents of spices, cinnamon and cardamom, a tantalizing whiff of honey. She prepared sweet rolls—a labor of love it was, meant for someone special. She couldn't wait to set them in front of him and see his dark eyes take light.

Still only half awake, she heard Mr. Saunders' feet hit the floor—his reactions outdistancing her own. By the time she crawled from her bed, wrapped herself in a shawl, and opened her door, he stood in the kitchen fully clothed, with his guns strapped on.

Did he sleep in those things?

He shot her one look before marching to the door and hauling it open. Whoever was busy beating on it abruptly halted.

"You Mr. Mountroy's guard? Come quick. Bank's being robbed!"

"Jesus," Mr. Saunders muttered, and rushed out the door.

Cissy stood there on her bare feet, the night air—for Mr. Saunders had failed to shut the door behind him—creeping across the floor. Her paralysis broke, and she hastily donned her shoes, wrapped the shawl more closely around her shoulders, and ran out the door in Mr. Saunders' wake.

Yes, it might be a foolish thing to do—darned foolish. If she had any common sense, she'd stay inside, lock the kitchen door up tight, and retreat to her room. Which just went to prove that Aunt Amelia had always been right about her, saying she had more guff than wisdom.

Outside, the air felt cool and it seemed very dark, even though the moon, just past full, sailed overhead and stared down at her like a cold, white eye. Cissy dashed around the side of the rooming house and started down Wylder Street. She could hear shouting—plenty of it—coming from farther down, and caught a glimpse of two figures ahead of her—Mr. Saunders, and whoever had fetched him.

Halfway down the street, where the bank stood, there were lights and more people, and horses. Her hair streaming out behind her, she ran on.

Suddenly, gunshots tore apart the fabric of the night—first just once, followed by a flurry of them. Cissy's feet dragged to a halt. She should flee. But she couldn't. She had to see what happened to Mr. Saunders.

That incredible thought rooted her where she stood. Perhaps fifty paces from the Goldmount Bank, she had a good view of everything.

Three horses milled in front of the bank along with a number of people. More folks spilled up from the back street, probably from the saloon that faced the railroad tracks there. Light shone from that direction, further illuminating the scene.

A figure lay on the boards in front of the bank.

Dead? Cissy stared, unable to tell. And Mr. Saunders—Mr. Saunders stood facing the bank, his whole body braced and both pistols in his hands.

"Come on out of there!" he roared, his voice tearing the night. "Do it slow."

Jesus, Jesus, bullets were going to fly. And here Cissy stood in her nightgown, making a perfect target. She needed to run. She needed to hit the dirt. But here she remained, unable to move.

Silly fool of a girl. She heard Aunt Amelia's voice in her mind, clear as a bell. What an awful thing to have ringing through her head, if she were about to die.

Light flickered from inside the bank, but nobody came out. Mr. Saunders took a few steps closer to the door, his movements careful and confident. He wouldn't go in there, would he? Nobody could be so brave.

All at once came a flurry of movement. The light inside the bank wavered, and three dark figures ran out. Gunfire once more erupted—two sharp, short shots. Cissy covered her ears with her hands as the first of the three figures fell. The folks watching the show from across the way all reacted, some shouting and some ducking back.

The first of the three figures had gone down not far from the man already sprawled on the ground. More shots and the second man clutched his shoulder and dropped the sack he carried.

The third man ducked, peeled off, and ran straight at Cissy.

Mr. Saunders spun. Both his guns remained in his hands and, even at this distance, Cissy could see the glitter in his eyes. He looked different—dangerous.

Deadly.

The third man—third bank robber—came pounding toward Cissy in a hard run, grunting and gasping. He ran away from the horses, away from Mr. Saunders, and had another sack under his arm.

And a drawn gun clutched in the other hand.

Somebody hollered. That was Mr. Saunders' voice. "Halt. Halt!"

Would he fire those guns again? Would the bullet hit Cissy instead of—

The fleeing man crashed into her with tremendous force. The impact drove the breath from her body and unlocked her knees. His arms caught at her, and one came across her like a bar. He turned them both to face Mr. Saunders.

"Back off!" he hollered.

Ah, God! Caught. She was caught.

Mr. Saunders stopped in his tracks, maybe fifty paces from them, his guns still at the ready. In the cold moonlight he looked emotionless and intent.

Cissy could smell the man who held her, a reek of sweat and leather. His arm was clamped over her breasts—a place no man had ever touched before. This certainly did not feel pleasant nor titillating.

"Back off," he grunted again. "Let me ride out and I won't have to hurt her."

"Let her go," Mr. Saunders returned. He sounded calm. Well, maybe not quite.

"I swear, I'll take 'er with me. A hostage."

Mr. Saunders took a step closer. The man holding Cissy fired his gun, the loudest thing she'd ever heard. She expected Mr. Saunders to fall, hit, but he kept on standing there.

The bullet must have missed.

Her eyes on Mr. Saunders' face, she jerked back, plowing her elbow into her captor's gut. At the same moment, her knees gave way. She sagged, and Mr. Saunders fired his pistol. Cissy felt the slug hit the man holding onto her. He grunted and tumbled back. She collapsed with him.

Everyone watching the scene exclaimed. Cissy, lying in the street with the moon shining in her eyes, wondered if the bullet had hit her after all.

Hands—gentle hands—touched her. Arms wrapped around her and lifted her up.

"You all right? Good God, Miss Cecilia, you're not—"

"Yes. Yes, I think I'm all right."

He touched her—he held her—Mr. Saunders did. It felt like heaven. Even at this awful moment, it was bliss, safety, and—oh, yes, there was the titillating pleasure.

His hands slid over her shoulders, her hair, as if to reassure himself. "He didn't hurt you any?"

"No." She looked down at the man sprawled on the ground. "Is he—"

Mr. Saunders let go of her. She wanted to cry out in protest but knew she couldn't possibly. He bent and touched the man on the ground, grunted, and kicked the gun away from his hand.

Folks streamed up to them, some carrying torches. In the flaring light, Mr. Saunders looked into Cissy's eyes. "What in hell were you doin' here?"

"You were here. I had to come."

****

Cissy's words made sense to Buck at the time.

Only later, when his heart stopped pounding and the fire in his blood died down, did he have a chance to think about them.

He'd seen Miss Cecilia off back to the rooming house in the company of Mrs. Culpepper, who soon came stumping down the street. That was after he'd assured himself Cissy truly was unhurt and he'd wrapped her shawl more closely around her slender shoulders with his own hands.

She wore a nightgown beneath that shawl, a pretty white thing. He, who in the past had paid ladies of the evening to strip for him, thought he'd moved beyond becoming hot over a cotton nightgown.

He hadn't.

After Cecilia left, he had to plow his way through the explanations. Mr. Mountroy arrived, along with several other business owners. Apparently the sheriff, a man named Hanson, was away from town just now, which might explain why the erstwhile bank robbers had chosen this moment for their attempt, but his deputy showed up, still only half dressed and looking unabashedly relieved he'd missed most of the fuss.

It turned out none of the would-be robbers was dead—all clean wounds, one in the arm, one in the side, and the one who'd been holding Miss Cecilia shot through the left shoulder.

"What a shot!" Mr. Mountroy roared while holding Buck's hand up in the air, like he'd won at fisticuffs or something. "Saved the bank and all you good folks' money."

Lloyd Winters, shot by one of the robbers, wasn't dead either, though he sure made a fuss when the town doctor knelt down over him and he came to. Hadn't the fellow ever taken a slug before? Why, Buck had been nicked and winged more times than he could call to mind.

The town doctor, a man called Sullivan, had turned out to assess the damages. He looked a lot different than any doc Buck had ever seen—tall and not very wordy, he appeared as tough as any gunfighter, and in fact wore a pistol strapped to his hip. But his hands moved competently over Winters, and he sure seemed to know what he was doing.

When all the excitement died down, when Lloyd had been taken away to the doc's premises and the robbers hauled off to jail, Mr. Mountroy led Buck inside the bank to his office.

"Sit down, son."

Son. Buck couldn't be twelve years younger than the other man.

Mr. Mountroy fished his flask out of the desk drawer. This time when he offered it, Buck accepted.

"See," Mr. Mountroy gloated, "this is why I hired you. This is precisely the reason, and what I called on you to do. Lloyd is worthless—"

"He did give the alarm."

"But he couldn't stop those bandits in their tracks the way you did, could he? Fine work. Fine work, indeed."

Buck didn't know what to say. If shooting men was fine work, he was a damned master crafter.

He'd wanted away from that life. It was why he came here to Wylder in the first place. Being a bank guard—well, it hadn't sounded like he'd be called upon to draw his guns.

Mr. Mountroy rubbed his chin. "I have to admit,

though, I'm surprised they tried to rob this place at night. Always before, they hit in daylight, when we're open. That's why I put you on days and Lloyd on the night shift."

"He won't be working for a while." The bullet Lloyd had taken was still lodged in his upper arm. Doc would probably be digging it out even now.

"Maybe I should put you on nights."

Buck's heart fell. If Mountroy did that, he'd have no choice but to eat supper with the other boarders, no excuse for those quiet, private moments in the kitchen with Miss Cecilia.

His pulse tripped as he remembered the moment when he'd turned and seen her standing there in the street, the hem of her nightgown lapping around her ankles and that pale hair streaming all around her. How wide her eyes had looked. She'd appeared like an angel.

You were here. I had to come. You were here, you were here. As if he mattered.

He scowled. An angel—for a devil like him?

He growled at Mountroy, "I sure can't work both days and nights."

"I never suggested it. Settle down, boy. I'll attribute your ill temper to shock."

Shock? Over winging a man? And don't call me 'boy.' Nobody but his father, the bastard, ever got away with that.

"I'm pleased, very pleased. It was a wise day when I contacted Pete, asking for a recommendation. And you, son, deserve a bonus." He reached into his vest pocket, pulled out a billfold, and extracted two bills, which he slid across the top of the desk. "Maybe you can move out of that old biddy's rooming house."

"I'm fine there." Buck didn't touch the money. Doing so would make him into what he was trying to stop being—a hired gun. Only, Mr. Mountroy had already hired him, hadn't he?

Mountroy shrugged. "Then kick up your heels at the saloon. Or the whorehouse."

Somewhat to his surprise, Buck discovered that prospect didn't appeal either.

Maybe—the mad idea occurred to him—he could take Miss Cecilia out for a nice meal. Probably not a good prospect—a man like him and a classy sort of woman like her.

When it came to Miss Cecilia Arkwright, though, there was something sharp and provoking underneath the class. He'd bet his life she wasn't all lady.

"Let me ask you, Mr. Mountroy, you know any place to get a fancy meal around here?"

Mountroy shrugged. "Most folks patronize Jake's Place. I, myself, have enjoyed a supper or two there."

Buck tucked the bills into his pocket, and fixed Mr. Mountroy with a hard stare. "And I'll just keep working days for now, right?"

"Uh—sure. Whatever you say."

Chapter Eight

Cissy endured not one but three separate lectures from Mrs. Culpepper, who chewed her up one side and down the other, denouncing her repeatedly for dashing out into the night—in her nightclothes, no less—and putting herself in harm's way.

"This isn't Chicago. Not that I'd expect you to run outside unclad there, either. Though Amelia did say you were shameless. And brazen. And disobedient."

Cissy had to confess she felt brazen every time she thought about Mr. Saunders putting his arms around her, the heat of his hands coming right through the thin fabric of her nightgown. She couldn't help but wonder how it would feel if the two of them were alone. If he touched her through her nightgown again and, maybe, pulled it off over her head, mussing her hair up so he had to run his fingers through it, and—

Yes, Aunt Amelia was right. She was shameless. But the idea of being in his company wearing nothing while he stood there all hard and masculine in his black leather…it made her tingle with heat.

Mercy, if one of her suitors back in Chicago had made her feel like this, she just might have accepted him.

But none of those men had dangerous black eyes, and dark hair long enough to tempt a woman's fingers to roam. None of them made her laugh. Or shot treacherous outlaws in the street, easy as if he did it every day.

That last point couldn't be good. Clearly, Mr. Saunders wasn't the sort of man with whom she should have an acquaintance.

She didn't see him until much later that day. She heard plenty about him, though—he and his fancy pistol work were all anybody wanted to discuss. People Mrs. Culpepper knew stopped by and gabbed about it, as did the delivery men and the boarders in the dining room.

"I was there and saw it all," said Kevin, the delivery boy who brought the milk. "That Mr. Saunders stayed cool. He was just like a gunslinger or something. A desperado."

Desperado.

Well, yes. There was something of the desperado about Mr. Saunders, and sad to say, it made Cissy's heart beat faster.

He never showed up for supper. She imagined that perhaps Mr. Mountroy from the bank had taken him to the saloon to toast his courage. She busied herself washing the dishes until a knock came at the back door. Before she could dry her hands, it opened a crack to reveal Mr. Saunders.

"Mind if I come in?"

"Of course not." Heat rushed through Cissy at the sight of him, black hair slicked back, handsome face—oh, yes, he was handsome—calm and composed. Pistols at his sides.

He came through and shut the door quietly. He didn't want Mrs. Culpepper to hear. Neither of them did.

"I'm afraid you missed supper."

"I know. Held up at the bank." His eyes crinkled. "Well, not held up—"

"I understand." She laughed softly. "I saved your helping. Just like always."

He ignored that. His dark eyes scoured her face before he asked, "You all right?"

"I have a couple bruises. Where I fell and—and where he grabbed me."

His eyes widened. "What were you doing there? Jesus, when I looked up and saw you, I—"

She'd already told him why she was there. Because he was. But no, it didn't make any sense. "I guess I just wanted to see what was going on."

He shook his head. "You never, never run toward gunfire."

"You did."

"That's different. I—I was acting in the performance of my job."

She allowed her gaze to consider him, lingering on the pistols at his sides. Tentatively, she pronounced, "You're a desperado, aren't you, Mr. Saunders?"

"How'd you come up with a word like that?"

"Everybody's saying it, all over town."

"Jesus." He toed out a chair with his boot and sat down. "That ain't good."

Cissy sat opposite him. "I suppose not."

"I came here to try and escape attention. For—for a new start."

"Mr. Saunders," Cissy wet her lips, "might I ask you something? Are you—are you in fact notorious?"

He raised his eyes to look at her. "What do you know about such things?"

"Even back east, we hear about the Wild West. Stories appear in the newspapers, About gunslingers. Men who—"

"Men who kill other men for money?" His eyes glittered. "What if I said it was true? What if I admitted I was such a man? Would you run away from me, Miss Cecilia?"

For the space of several heartbeats, they gazed at one another. Heat swept upward into Cissy's face. She shook her head.

He didn't move. "What would you do?"

She sucked in a breath. "I might get up and fetch you your supper. I might sit here and talk with you while you ate."

"But I would think, Miss Cecilia, such a confession might well change everything."

"Everything's already changed. You saved my life last night, with your skill at shooting. So it seems I should be glad you possess such an ability."

He blinked at her.

"Maybe one day you'll see fit to tell me your story. Meanwhile, I can keep my mouth shut. Do you want that supper?"

"I do. Thank you kindly."

She sat back down with him while he ate, letting the dish water cool and the suds die. She watched his hands, which moved with such careful grace, and thought about them on her skin. At first, they spoke of nothings—the weather, the work she did around the house, and how boring his job at the bank was, usually. Then he asked her to tell him a little something about Andy, and she shared the concerns prompted by his letter.

"He's a good boy. Always showed promise with his lessons. Uncle Benjamin wants to train Andy up to follow him in our father's business. I think that's why he took us in after our parents died. He never had a son of his own. But there's something amiss. I thought so, even before they sent me away. Now that Andy thinks so too…"

"Maybe that's why they sent you away." Mr. Saunders dug into the slice of triple-layer cake she'd saved for him. "I've found if there's a bad smell, well, there's usually a carcass someplace."

Cissy rested her chin on her hand. "I did think of that, yes. I've written to my father's lawyer, but I'm not sure he's on the up-and-up either. How can I protect Andy from so far away? I have only my suspicions, and no proof. If I bring Andy out here to join me, will I be depriving him of a really fine opportunity? And I have no way to support him out here—not yet."

"You said he's getting a fine education there in Chicago."

"The best. My father insisted on that for both of us."

He cocked an eye at her. "Education's a grand thing." His expression became unreadable. "My father, believe it or not, was a well-educated man."

"Why wouldn't I believe that? You're well spoken."

"I was a bitter disappointment to him. He had a decided way of handling his disappointment. I left home just as soon as I could carry a gun."

"Really?"

"Yes, ma'am."

"How old were you?"

"Fourteen."

"Goodness! Andy's only eight. I'd hate to think of him on his own."

"He'll never have to worry about that. He's got you."

"That's nice of you to say, but as I've had eternally drummed into me, and as I proved over again last night, I'm reckless and unreliable. I make poor decisions. I'm not good for him."

"You love him, don't you?" Mr. Saunders' eyes met Cissy's. "Never underestimate the value of being loved. You don't know what it's worth till you have to try and live without it."

Chapter Nine

Cissy dreamed about Mr. Saunders that night. She dreamed she got up and, still clad in her nightclothes, left her room and walked next door to his. She dreamed he woke up as she stood beside his bed where he lay with the blanket pulled up over a broad, naked chest. When he opened his eyes and looked at her, she drew the nightgown off over her head.

So real did it seem, she came awake gasping and damp with sweat. Heat suffused her, triggered by the look in his dark eyes when she bared herself for him. She groped her hands all over her body, desperate to make sure she remained in her bed, and clothed.

What was the matter with her? Despite all the insults Aunt Amelia had hurled at her, she was a decent young woman, was she not? Raised proper. And her impulses, while sometimes undisciplined, had never leaned in *that* direction.

Of course, she'd never before ventured into the Wild West, where men shot each other in the street and life hung by a thread.

Who knew what path her impulses might take her? Who knew what she might start wanting, faced with a man like Burt Saunders?

Still, she shocked herself. And she had trouble looking him in the eye during breakfast the next morning, where the talk was still all about the attempted bank robbery. The other boarders took the opportunity to ask Mr. Saunders questions about what had happened while Mrs. Culpepper reigned over the head of the table. Cissy listened as she carried platters in and out.

Mr. Saunders answered everyone's questions quietly, in a way that didn't tell a lot. The three bandits, it seemed, had been patched up by the town doctor and would all survive. They were being held till they could be taken to Cheyenne for trial.

Said sour-faced Mr. Jacobs, "I'm relieved to know we have a proper guard at the bank, who can keep our money safe."

After the meal, Cissy began ferrying platters back out to the kitchen. She started when she discovered Mr. Saunders had followed her there.

"Oh, good morning." Heat stained her skin.

"Morning, Miss Cecilia." He shifted his weight from one leg to the other, and she stepped aside, assuming he needed something from his room before leaving the boarding house. He already wore his pistols and held his black hat in his hands, by the brim.

He didn't move past her, though. "Is something amiss, Miss Cecilia?"

"No. Why should you ask?"

"You haven't so much as looked at me this morning."

She swiped at a few strands of hair that had come loose from the bun at the back of her neck, and trailed down her cheek. "I'm merely very busy."

"Glad to hear I haven't offended in some way. I'm hoping we're still friends."

Friends. Ah, yes. And one did not strip off her nightgown for a friend, even in a dream.

She laid down the plates she held, and looked him in the face. Dark eyes considered her with a steady regard she had no hope of escaping. Mercy! What was she to do with these feelings?

A smile quirked one corner of his mouth. His expression softened. "You work far too hard, Miss Cecilia."

"It's probably good for my soul. Redemption for my sins and all that."

"I doubt very much you've committed many sins."

"You'd be surprised."

"Of course, friends—friends tend to forgive each other those kinds of transgressions."

"So they do."

He shifted again. "I'd like to ask you something. All this while, you've been saving my supper for me, with no reward. Would you allow me to buy you some, in return?"

"I beg your pardon?"

"I apologize, Miss Cecilia, for not making myself clear. I'm asking you to go to supper with me."

Her eyes widened in astonishment. "Go to supper? Where?"

"Mr. Mountroy tells me there's a good restaurant in town, called Jake's."

"Yes. Yes, there is. But why would you—" She stopped abruptly.

"I guess I'm still not making myself clear. I'd like you to walk out with me."

Oh.

Heat rushed through Cissy again. Mrs. Culpepper would go mad over this. She'd write to Aunt Amelia, who would deride her all over again.

Might be a good reason to accept his offer. Then again, the fact that she wanted to take her clothes off for the man might make a good reason to refuse.

The light in his eyes dimmed. “If you don’t like the notion—”

“I didn’t say that, Mr. Saunders.” She lifted her chin. “I do like the notion, very much. I’m just thinking, well, whether I’m willing to start something.”

He shrugged. “I’m just proposing supper. Not marriage.”

Cissy laughed. “True.” She held out her hand. “Then I accept. When did you have in mind?”

“How about tonight, after you finish here?”

“Yes.”

He enfolded her work-roughened hand in his calloused one. “I’ll look forward to it.”

“Shall we—shall we meet at the restaurant?”

“No. I’ll escort you from here, right and proper.”

Heavens! There was nothing proper about any of this.

He released her hand and strode off into his room. Cissy remained where she was, wondering if she’d just made the worst mistake of her life. Dinner—with a man like that! Ah, well, when in Wylder, Wyoming, why not go ahead and take a walk on the wild side?

****

I’m just proposing supper. Not marriage. What sort of a damn fool thing had that been to say? The words haunted Buck all day long, while he fielded endless questions at the bank, endured stares from townsfolk who seemingly came by just to gape at him. While he talked to Mr. Mountroy and caught the admiring glances of any ladies who passed. And oh, yeah, those were admiring glances, without a doubt.

Maybe he'd do better to spend his bonus at a place like the Wylder County Social Club rather than start something with Miss Cecilia Arkwright. That's how she thought of it—starting something.

Truth be told, so did he. And he wanted to start something with her. It wasn't just that he found her attractive—though he did. It was the glint in those blue eyes of hers that drew him, and the way they were able to laugh together. Laughter as easy as that was rare.

If he were honest—and he wanted always to be honest with her, another rarity—he'd trade a hundred nights at the Social Club for one kitchen table conversation with her.

I'm proposing supper. Not marriage. Not yet—but the idea had appeared, for the first time ever, in his mind. He must be crazy. Even having been disposed of by her family like so much dirty laundry, Cecilia was far too good for him. If the truth about his identity came to light, he'd have to hightail it out of here—or face off against some other gunslinger with ambitions.

Maybe he should tell her the truth about his identity. She had a good brain in that flaxen head of hers. She deserved a chance to make up her own mind about him.

The day dragged even more than usual, because he knew he had something good at the end of it. Would Mrs. Culpepper forbid Cecilia from seeing him? Could she? Would the two of them, dining right out in the open this way, prompt more talk in town?

After work he returned to the boarding house, stepped in through the back door, and froze, feeling just like he'd been punched in the gut.

She'd dressed up. She'd dressed up *for him*.

She wore a stylish green gown with white lace at the cuffs and throat—nothing like her usual skirt and blouse—and a green hat that sat at a sweet angle on her head. She'd wound her tow-colored hair all up in the back, beneath the brim, and looked so sophisticated Buck nearly fled.

Nearly.

Only he couldn't, because his heart was caught. Right at that moment, it was. He felt it happen, just as if she'd reached her fingers into his chest and claimed it for her own.

He puffed out a breath. "Why, Miss Cecilia. Well, look at you!"

"My traveling clothes, from back home."

"You look mighty fine. Did you tell Mrs. Culpepper you're walking out?"

She tipped up that dangerous chin of hers. "I did not. I've finished my chores, and I figure the rest of the evening is my own."

"Uh—just let me wash up. I won't keep you waiting long."

He went into his room, shut the door, and leaned against it. Damn it all, what had just happened? Was he truly planning to walk out with that lovely woman on his arm?

Hell, yes.

He poured water from the jug into the wash basin, ducked his head, and stripped off his shirt. He'd need a clean one and—and maybe his best jacket. Yeah, for sure, the jacket.

The jacket was black broadcloth with long tails in the back. He added a string tie and squinted into the shaving mirror that hung on the wall. Not good enough, but the best he could do.

He should have brought her flowers or something. But where did a man get flowers in a place like Wylder?

He went back out, his hair still damp, and offered Miss Cecilia his arm. When she took it, he quivered from head to toe.

Chapter Ten

"Miss Cecilia, I want to be honest with you."

The dinner—not half as fancy at Buck could have wished—was over. They'd endured the curiosity of the lady who waited on them and the avid stares of all the other diners. Some folks had come in after them, just to stare, or so it seemed.

Cissy leaned her chin on her hand in that way she had and looked at him with her fine blue eyes. It made him feel like the only man in the world. "I wish you would. Be honest with me, I mean."

Buck drew a breath, tore his gaze from hers, and glanced around the restaurant. "Maybe best not said here. Would you like to go walking?"

"Yes. It's a lovely evening." She stayed where she was, seated, till he pulled out her chair. Like they were a regular couple or something.

Outside, her words proved true, though he'd barely noticed the weather beforehand. A moon on its way to the last quarter sailed overhead, and the air smelled of something besides dust and horseshit.

They walked in silence a few moments, with her arm curled around his. It felt—good, too good for words.

He began, "Miss Cecilia—"

She said at the same instant, "Do you think—" She broke off before adding, "Please, say what you wish."

What did she want to ask him? Did he ever think? About her? Constantly. “I have a confession to make.”

“Oh?” She glanced up into his face. “Better make it, then. Friends don’t keep secrets from one another.”

“Nope, I guess they don’t.” He sucked in a breath. “I’d like you to know, Burt Saunders isn’t my real name.”

“Burt? So, that’s your given name?” she sounded surprised.

“No, that’s what I’m sayin’. It’s not. My name’s not Burt, it’s Buck.”

“Buck.”

“Buckminster Delham Standish.”

“Well, that’s a mouthful.”

“I’m known as Buck Standish. You ever hear of me?”

“No, I’m afraid not.”

She wouldn’t, being from the East.

“Are you famous?”

“Notorious. Just like you said before. Well known as a gunslinger. A hired gun.”

She stumbled and stopped walking. They were half way down Wylder Street, with buildings on both sides.

“A desperado. You’re a desperado. I knew it.”

Seems she had. “How?”

“Just a feeling.” She shivered.

“Well, Miss Cecilia, if we’re going to stay friends, I figure there are some things you have a right to know about me.”

“Are you wanted?”

He shifted uncomfortably. “In some parts of the country. Not here. But—”

“We can’t talk in the middle of the street. Come

on." She seized his hand and towed him off between two buildings and toward the open country beyond. Dark found them there, and when she paused beneath a tree to face him, he could barely see her expression.

"Tell me. Tell me everything."

Not everything. Not that. "Men like me, we tend to get a reputation. In all justice, we earn that reputation. Other men—the ones who want to prove themselves, to test how fast they are with a gun—come looking for us. When those fellows challenge me, I'm obligated to face off with them."

She blinked up at him. "You've killed men?"

"I have. I surely have, though it was always in a fair fight. Men call me out, I answer the call. Somebody hires me to take somebody else on—I always do call that fellow out when I find him, and it's a duel. I've never shot a man in the back, and never will."

She shivered again, where she stood. Or was that a shudder? She'd let go of his hand now and backed off a step. His heart sank.

Doggedly, he went on, "I figure it might happen again. Folks find out who I am, men will come looking to challenge me. Somebody here in town recognizes me, word will get out. I thought you deserved to know that, before we—if we should—decide to stay friends. I come with a pack of trouble."

"I see." She appeared to think about that, gnawing on her lip, and Buck felt his world begin to crash around him. What had he been doing? Living in a dream, that was what. Imagining a lady like Cecilia could form any kind of liking for a fellow like him. For, whatever else she might be, with that spark of daring in her eyes, and despite her family having sent her away, she was still every inch the lady.

"Well, so you came to Wylder and changed your name, hoping for a new start?"

"I did. This friend of mine, Pete Beckinstall—I traveled with him when I first left home—is an acquaintance of Mr. Mountroy's, at the bank. And since I'm not as well known here in Wyoming Territory as in some other places, he suggested I take the position of bank guard."

"And you think you can leave that other life behind?"

"I want to, Miss Cecilia. I'm almost thirty years old, and I've spent half my life on the move. It's no way to live. A man's got to put down roots eventually."

She spread her arms. "And you choose to put them down here?"

Should Buck say what he wanted to say? That when he'd come to Wylder, he'd thought it didn't matter, that one western town was like another. But now—well, she was here, and that made all the difference.

"It's a good town. I could see myself staying, if—" His throat closed up on him.

"If you don't get discovered?"

"Right, yes."

"Thank you, Mr.—Saunders—for trusting me with your confidence."

"I thought it's only fair. That you know who and what you're dealing with, I mean. If you decide you no longer want to keep up our acquaintance—well, I'll understand."

She stood there thinking about it for a moment that lasted forever, the dark washing all the color out of her green dress and the lace at her throat gleaming. Buck told himself to take her decision on the chin. He'd suffered a lot of losses in the past. His ma and little newborn sister, both together. Any friends he'd made, when Pa hauled them west. His sister, Abby, when he left home at fourteen. His conscience. Not his pride, though. Surely that would keep him standing here, straight and tall. He was what he was. He'd changed what he could, but for the most part he was prideful and strong, fast with a gun. She'd have to accept that, or leave it.

At last she spoke, her voice low and melodious in the dark. "You're not a cruel man, are you, Mr. Saunders?"

"What's that?"

"You don't beat your horse or kick stray dogs, or pistol-whip hapless drunks?"

"No, ma'am. I can honestly say I've never done any of those things."

"Good, because I cannot abide cruelty."

Buck quivered where he stood.

Slowly, she stepped toward him. Her hands came up, looking like two white birds, and fluttered toward the front of his coat.

"But I do respect honesty in a man. And I value the company of a man I respect."

He caught her hands in his and clasped them tight. He wanted to hold her, wanted it so bad he hurt. Against all the odds and likelihoods, he wanted her in his life.

His fool mouth went on talking. "Just so you know, I've never been what you'd call lucky." Till now. "If my usual luck holds out, somebody will show up here in Wylder to call me out."

"That would be a darned shame."

"You're right. It would. Either way, Miss Cecilia, I'd like to thank you for giving me a chance."

"Seems to me we're both misfits, in a way. Washed up on the shore here in Wylder. Least we can do is walk a ways together."

"I appreciate that, I surely do. If there's anything else you'd like to ask me—" He frowned. "In fact, there was something you started to ask me, right? If I thought—?"

She took a step closer and lifted her face to his in the gloom. "I was going to say, do you think people are sometimes just destined to be together?"

Buck's throat went dry. "Like—?"

"Like, they just happen to meet, tossed up on the shores of Wylder, Wyoming maybe, and out of a world of people, they mesh? Their thoughts, and their conversation. What they think's amusing. What they feel is right."

"Well, Miss Cecilia," he drew her clear up against him, "that would be something beyond happenstance, wouldn't it? That would be something on the order of a miracle."

"It would." She freed her hands from his and laid them against his chest as if—as if she claimed him or something, before gripping the lapels of his coat. He bent his head at the same instant she stretched up to him. Their lips met.

Buck had never before kissed a lady. Plenty of whores, yes. Pete had treated him to his first at sixteen, when he got what Pete called the itch. What he felt for Cecilia was nothing like that. He liked and, yes, respected her. She delighted him in a way he couldn't hope to explain. Yet as soon as their lips met, the heat came rushing. Holy hell, this thing between them—it was a powder keg.

A gentleman, or so he imagined, should bestow upon a lady a chaste kiss. A mark of regard, maybe. He shouldn't use the pressure of his lips to part hers. He shouldn't take the little moan that came from her throat as encouragement, and he definitely shouldn't taste her with his tongue. That just wasn't respectable. It wasn't. And Miss Cecilia was a lady.

Then again, a lady probably shouldn't lean against him this way, as if she couldn't get close enough, or meet his tongue with her own. Stroke it a bit, and invite him deeper in. She should be shocked by his boldness.

Shouldn't she?

Who cared? As his English father might have said, who the hell bloody cared?

Too late to try and hold back now. Buck threw caution to the winds and kissed Miss Cecilia. He kissed her deep, as if he searched for something—her soul, maybe. He kissed her long, as if he wanted something.

Forever, maybe.

Could he have forever, a man like him? That thought startled him so much, he halted the kiss, reining himself in abruptly. She gasped, gasped and clung to him, still hanging onto his lapels as if she'd never let go.

He had to say something. Apologize, yeah, that was it. Apologize for taking such liberties. But his brain felt blasted, like that powder keg had gone off.

She spoke first. "Why, Mr. Saunders—"

"That isn't my name. Buck, call me Buck." He said

it desperately, as if yes, he wanted her to claim him.

"Buck. Buckminster." Amusement filled her voice. That seduced him as much as her kiss. Just imagine having that sharp bit of humor to fill his days.

"Right. Buckminster." He wrapped his arms around her and pulled her closer, so she could feel all of him.

"You make me tingle. Right down to my toes." Of all the things she might say, he hadn't expected that. She laid her cheek against his shoulder. It turned out to be one of the best sensations ever.

He mused, "I don't suppose we can stand here like this all night." No. He could take her back to the boarding house. Sneak her into his room, right next to hers. Cajole her out of that pretty green dress and put his hands all over her soft skin.

No, no. Wouldn't be respectable.

"I suppose not. But we've more or less vowed to always tell each other the truth. And truth is, I sure did enjoy that kiss. Fact is, I'd enjoy another one."

This time she kissed him. She did it tentatively, as if she hadn't kissed a lot of men. And that was all right, because the heat came even faster this time, and her tongue teased his lips, seeking gentle admittance before she stepped away from him.

Not far. She didn't step far, and she kept her grip on his coat. "In the interest of truth, Buckminster, I have to tell you, you smell very good. And taste even better."

"As do you, Miss Cecilia."

"Call me Cissy. Everybody I care for does."

Everybody I care for.

Not a man easily felled or shaken, Buck

nevertheless felt himself fall. There in the dark, he took her hand in his.

"Then, Miss Cissy, let me see you safe home."

Chapter Eleven

After that, Cissy pretty much dominated Buck's thoughts. All day long, while at his post, she kept him company, sharing that smile of hers—the one that made the wicked light appear in her eyes—and whispering soft words in his ear. He found it a powerful distraction and, more than once, had to order himself to pay attention to what went on in the street. He had to focus his eyes over and over again.

He did take notice two days later, in the middle of the afternoon, when a man rode up on a tall, dusty horse. Both the man and the horse looked weary, and the rider didn't push the pace, making Buck think they'd covered some distance since morning.

As every afternoon, folks thronged the street in front of the bank. Buck, who unlike Lloyd Winters didn't like availing himself of the chair on the boards there, had little to do but pace the perimeter of the building and keep watch.

He'd begun learning the rhythm of Wylder—the times of day families or hands might ride in from outlying ranches, the moments things tended to grow rowdy. The chances for trouble brewing.

This man didn't look like trouble, but he did have what Buck's father would have called a measure of *gravitas.*

You know what that word means, Buckminster? It

means weight. A demand for respect. Unexpectedly, he heard his father's voice in his mind. *You pay attention to such men, if you know what's good for you.*

Jesus, Buck thought, blinking at the man on the tall horse. Would he never get that damned voice out of his head?

This man looked to be in his late fifties, well-weathered, with a seamed, deeply tanned face and keen eyes. He steered his mount to the hitching post in front of the sheriff's office across from the bank, but not till he'd taken a good, long look at Buck, where he stood.

The missing sheriff, most likely.

The man tied up his mount and, sure enough, went inside the sheriff's office. Soon a younger man came out and led his horse away, followed not long after by the original rider, who crossed the street to Buck.

And yes, he wore a star pinned to his vest. Eyes the color of the far, blue distances inspected Buck up and down with considerable care.

Buck stiffened. If anyone in Wylder had a chance of recognizing him, it would be this man. Wanted posters of Buck did exist—he'd seen one. Fortunately, it didn't look much like him, but this fellow appeared nobody's fool. And he wore his gun low, the same way Buck did.

"You Burt Saunders?"

"I am." Several possible scenes rushed through Buck's mind. An arrest. A wild escape and flight from town. No, that wouldn't work—he couldn't leave without Midnight.

He couldn't leave without seeing Miss Cecilia again, either. Damn it, he wanted another piece of her pie.

He wanted another kiss.

"Earl Hanson. Sheriff." Hanson jerked a thumb at the star pinned to his chest. "Can I have a few minutes of your time?"

"I'm on duty here. Guard."

"I know." Hanson stepped past him, opened the door of the bank and bellowed inside. "Fred? I'm borrowing your man here a few minutes. All right?"

He then jerked his head at Buck, indicating the office across the street.

A man of few words was Earl Hanson, apparently.

Buck accompanied him, not without reservations. Inside the office, conditions appeared utilitarian at best. A desk faced the door, a few wooden chairs lined up opposite it. Against the rear wall had been built two cells, both empty at the moment.

Buck wrinkled his nose involuntarily. Such places had a smell—and he'd been in enough of them to know. He'd spent time in pens just like these, and broken out of some.

"Sit down, Saunders." Hansen took the chair behind the desk with a weary grunt.

"Is there a problem?" Buck asked cautiously, standing where he was.

Hanson inspected him again, taking his time with it, gaze lingering on Buck's guns. Buck didn't think he was eagle-eyed enough to see the initials carved on them, but if he did, Buck's game would be up.

"Don't expect so. Just wanted a word with you about what happened t'other night."

Buck had shot three men. He sat down and did his best to appear indifferent.

"Where you from, Mr. Saunders?"

"Here and there. Been kicking around for some time."

"Where from, most recently?"

"Been working some ranches up in big sky country. Security, mostly." Hopefully, that would be beyond this man's territory.

Hanson nodded. "According to what my deputy told me when I got in, you're damned good at it."

Buck shrugged. "It suits me."

"How did you come to get hooked up with Fred Mountroy?"

"Mutual acquaintance referred me."

Hanson grimaced, his lined face breaking up into a thousand wrinkles. The keen eyes didn't leave Buck's face. "Fred's had a succession of guards, and so far none of 'em's been a lick of good. The bank's been robbed twice. He tell you that?"

"Yes, sir."

"Nobody's been able to stop bandits from walking in there and taking what they wanted—till now."

Buck shrugged.

"My deputy tells me you weren't even on duty when it happened."

"No, sir."

"First time there's been a robbery at night."

"So I'm led to understand."

"Let me say this, Saunders. Wylder is a curious sort o' place. Do you know how it was founded? The Wylder family, them that run the mercantile, were traveling west and decided this was a good place to settle. God knows why. They wanted a quiet life, but things don't always go the way you want."

"No, sir, they do not."

"Other folks came, not all of them peaceful homesteaders." Hanson waved an arm. "You see what I deal with out there. Every manner of customer, from families to—well, gunslingers." His eyes glinted steel. "The town wants to be respectable, and that's a problem, given it's at odds with some of those who come here."

"It's a fine ambition, though."

"Yep. A town—or a man—can have ambitions. Had 'em myself, once upon a time, and I know what it is to turn from using my gun for harm to using it to keep the peace. Now, them guns of yours—"

Buck stiffened.

"—they look well used, and you're good with 'em. How do I know you won't give me any trouble?"

"Me taking on those bank robbers might be an indication."

"Men are funny, almost as much so as towns. They can play at one thing, and be something else again. Why, a man might protect what's in that bank just so he can steal it later on."

"I'm no bank robber, Sheriff Hanson."

"I don't think you're an ordinary bank guard, either."

Buck drew a breath. "You have an objection to me working for Mr. Mountroy?"

"Fred can hire who he likes. And in this instance, you could say he's had a good result. What I'm telling you, Saunders, is I don't need any more strife. Keeping this town peaceable is difficult enough. I'm dealing with ornery mountain men, restless ranch hands, and men who, on a Friday night, drink way too much. I'm away from town far too often, overseeing a territory that's just plain too big. I need another deputy but can't find anybody decent. Like I said, I don't need complications from somebody who might—or might not—be a bank guard."

Buck looked Hanson in the eye. "Sounds like maybe you're looking to retire."

"Maybe I am. But my first loyalty's to Wylder, and the Wylder family."

"Sheriff, you won't get any trouble out of me."

"Glad to hear it. Because, Mr. Saunders, I deal with trouble swift and hard."

"I'm just here looking for a quiet life."

Hanson's gaze dropped once more to Buck's guns. "I hope so."

"Can I go now? Back to my post?"

"Sure, son."

Buck rose.

"Oh, Mr. Saunders, I thought you'd like to know, those three men you corralled on my behalf have been taken to the circuit judge at Cheyenne. Turns out they're well known." He gestured at a pile of papers on a table against the wall. "See all those posters and bulletins? We get them all the time, about wrongdoers."

Buck's heart sank, though he strove to keep it from showing. "That's an awful lot of information to plow through."

"It's damn near impossible. Some men, though, have a smell about 'em. And some, I come to just recognize by type. Gunslingers, for instance, have a certain appearance."

"Lots of men carry guns."

"You're right." Hanson gave a laugh. "Includin' our doc."

"And even a gunfighter," Buck added with deliberation, "might want a chance to settle down—say, maybe, in a town like this."

Hanson shrugged. "Live and let live, that's what I say. I tend to judge a man by his actions."

"That's a fine philosophy."

Steel once more glinted in the sheriff's eye. "And if his actions turn bad, well—then I have to hope I'm still fast enough."

Chapter Twelve

Cissy heard it first in the dining room—the name Buck Standish—and it stopped her cold. Supper had ended. As usual, Buck hadn't showed. Cissy put his supper aside with her own, looking forward to those moments when they'd be able to sit together at the kitchen table and talk. She began ferrying the plates out of the dining room.

"Buck Standish. A gunslinger."

Her head turned. She wasn't sure who'd spoken the name, maybe Mr. Petrie, with his withered lips and pinched face.

Mrs. Culpepper raised her eyebrows. "Surely not. Here in my house? An outlaw?"

Cissy paused with her back to the kitchen door.

Mr. Tyler said, "It's just a rumor, Mrs. Culpepper. I'm sure it's not true. Just the sort of thing folks say."

"Though," Mr. Cuslow put in, "your newest boarder is awful good with those guns of his."

"Heavens!" Mrs. Culpepper fanned herself with her napkin.

"And he sure weren't a-scared to face off against them bank robbers," Mr. Petrie contributed.

"Who said this? Called him—Buck Standish?" Mrs. Culpepper demanded.

"I heard it from a fellow who overheard some speculation in the saloon."

Mrs. Culpepper planted her nose in the air. "No more than drunken gossip, then? Probably not true, but I shall certainly speak to Mr. Saunders about it, just as soon as he comes in. Notorious is he, this Standish fellow?"

"Real notorious, Mrs. Culpepper. Who knows how many men he's gunned down?"

Cissy pushed through into the kitchen where she stood stock still, heat washing over her in a wave. Buck needed to be warned. As soon as he came through the door, Mrs. Culpepper would likely pounce on him, looking for answers.

She dumped the dirty dishes in the sink and, not even pausing to grab her shawl, ran out the back door.

Wylder, as she'd learned, was an odd kind of place—quiet and mostly law-abiding during the day, it tended to take on a different demeanor at night when the saloon and other establishments came to life. This current hour was the in-between time when respectable people went home to their supper and the rowdier residents came into their own.

She saw Buck coming down the street before she'd gone fifty paces, knew him from his height and the way he walked, all hard-held confidence. Suddenly she could taste him on her tongue and closed her mind fiercely to the sensation. Not now.

When he got near enough, she saw he wore a grim expression. And folks watched him down the street, while pretending they didn't.

Had he already heard what she needed to tell him?

They met, and she fought the urge to reach out and touch him. Too many eyes watching them.

"Miss Cecilia." His gaze moved past her to the

boarding house. “Something wrong?”

“No—maybe yes. I wanted a word with you. I’ve just heard a certain name bandied about in Mrs. Culpepper’s dining room.”

His fine lips tightened. “I’m not surprised. Seems someone’s recognized me—or fancies he did. It’s all over town.”

Cissy’s heart fell to her knees. “Oh, no.”

“Of course, the fellow might be mistaken. Then again, he might not.”

“I wanted to warn you, Mrs. Culpepper intends to question you about—well, about your identity when you get home.”

“I see.”

“Do you think she’ll toss you out?”

“I hope not.”

“Me, too.” Panic fluttered in Cissy’s throat. She couldn’t lose him when she’d barely found him. She reached for his arm.

Carefully, he put both his hands behind him. “Folks watching, Miss Cissy.”

“Right. You’re right.” She twined her fingers together. “You—you won’t leave Wylder, will you?”

“I sure don’t want to.” He focused on her face. “Don’t want to gun down anyone else, either. But if someone comes looking for me—”

“I understand.” She truly was walking on the wild side. And that scared her more than a little.

Was this the path for her, stepping out with a gunman, someone other men came hunting down?

He began walking again. She kept pace with him. After a moment, just as if he read her mind, he said, “You know, Miss Cissy, I’d sure understand if you wanted to part ways with me."

Part ways? Cissy pressed her lips together. "Is that how friends treat each other, Buck?"

"I reckon not. But—"

"You already confided in me who and what you are. I chose to remain friends with you anyway." Only, friends didn't kiss that way, as if they wanted to consume each other.

"Yeah, but I thought you might want a chance to choose again, now that my past looks set to catch up with me." They'd nearly reached the rooming house. He paused and looked at her, his dark eyes shaded. "Makes it risky. And you have your little brother to worry about. If you mean to make a life here, for you and maybe him, you'll need to be careful what company you keep."

Did she mean to make a life here? Rather shockingly, Cissy found that might depend on where Buckminster Standish would be.

"I haven't yet decided what's best for Andy. I sure would like to get him away from Aunt Amelia. But there are opportunities for him in Chicago."

Buck swallowed something that looked bitter. "Might be better opportunities there for you, too. God knows, I can't ever offer you anything—"

She put her hands on her hips. "You telling me to go home?"

"No." His lips quirked. "Hell, no." He glanced at the house. "You go on in the back, so nobody knows we've been together."

"The whole town knows we've been together. Half of them saw us at Jake's."

"Still, I'll go in the front, face the music."

"Good luck." She ached to touch him—on the hand, on the arm. She wanted to lean up and kiss him on the cheek. Instead, like the skivvy Mrs. Culpepper would make of her, she scuttled off through the back door and returned to her sink, heaped with dishes.

****

"She threw you out?" Cecilia's beautiful eyes widened and a flush came to her cheeks. She looked lovely, and dauntingly angry. It shook Buck to the heart that she should get so upset on his behalf.

They'd met in the kitchen when he came through to pack up his belongings. Must be she hadn't heard the words he shared with Mrs. Culpepper, who'd greeted him on the front stoop and barred his way.

"You can gather your things and leave. Your stay here at Culpepper's is done." Part of the reason, so Mrs. Culpepper insisted, was Cecilia. "Mr. Saunders—or whatever your real name is—I have a young lady in this house. One gently raised. And her quarters are right beside your own. It's not respectable, and I won't countenance it."

Buck couldn't blame the woman. Miss Cecilia had a reputation to guard. But gazing into her face now, his spirits plummeted. "Cissy, I can't stay. The only reason she's let me in is to get my things—and leave. In fact, I'm sure she'll be on my heels any minute."

Cissy laid her fingers, wet and soapy, on his arm. "Where will you go?" The distress in her eyes deepened.

"I figure I'll bed down at the stable for a few nights. I'm already paying for Midnight's keep, and I reckon Mr. Daniels won't mind."

"In a stable? But—"

"Believe me, Miss Cissy, I've slept in worse places."

"But it's not right. I tell you what. I'll still hold your meals for you. After Mrs. Culpepper's asleep, I want you to come around back here and—"

The door to the dining room crashed open. Mrs. Culpepper came through like a ship in full sail, her indignant bosom leading the way. "Cecilia, what did I tell you about speaking to this man?"

"He's a boarder, Mrs. Culpepper."

"Not any longer. I've asked him to leave. This house does not welcome louts and outlaws."

Cissy turned to face her. "Three days ago, he was a hero."

"New information has come to light. He," Mrs. Culpepper pointed at Buck dramatically, "is said to be a desperate gunslinger. Now, I will give you the benefit of the doubt and assume you did not know that. But I owe it to your aunt to keep you safe from unsavory influences. So far as I'm aware, you are still a young woman of virtue."

Cissy's cheeks burned with a combination of anger and embarrassment. But Buck did not give her a chance to reply.

He tipped his hat, stepped away from her and made for his room. "Ma'am."

He didn't have much to pack up. He'd barely settled here. Except his heart—his heart had settled, in spite of his native caution, and he could feel it starting to bleed as he yanked up the roots.

All the while he threw things into his saddlebags, he could hear the two women arguing in the kitchen. Miss Cissy tried to defend him—pointed out it wasn't fair to judge somebody by what people said about him. It didn't get her very far.

When he opened the door and stepped out, he saw she had tears in her eyes.

He couldn't bear that. He'd borne a lot of things in his time. The death of his ma. His father's drinking and snide remarks, the way he talked Buck down. Nothing unusual there—Oliver Standish had talked everyone down. He talked himself up real easy, but when he picked up the strap and beat his son, accompanying each blow with an insult, Buck saw what he was.

He'd endured all that. He couldn't withstand Cissy's tears.

"Good evening, ladies." He went out quickly, before his heart could urge him to stay, before he said something stupid or made promises he could not keep.

He knew when he wasn't wanted. He always had.

Chapter Thirteen

Cissy next heard the name Buck Standish when Mrs. Culpepper sent her on an errand to the mercantile. It seemed to be on everyone's lips now, just as if folks didn't have anything else to talk about.

Two women gossiped on the boardwalk outside the store, standing in the warm sunshine, their expressions avid. As Cissy passed them, one confided in the other, "My man says it'll all come down to a gunfight. With men like Buck Standish, it always does."

If somebody calls me out, I'll face him.

Cissy hurried on by, but the interior of the store proved no different. The proprietor stood deep in conversation with a male customer, and while Cissy waited her turn, she couldn't help but hear what they discussed.

"Now that word's out he's here in Wylder, it won't take long for somebody to show up, gunning for him."

"You certain sure he is Buck Standish?" the proprietor asked doubtfully.

"Seems so. One of the hands from Blake's ranch caught a glimpse of him. Says he saw Buck Standish out California way two years ago. It's him."

The proprietor looked shocked. "Well, I have to say I'm not prepared for gunfights in the street right in front of my shop. Wylder's a respectable town."

"Don't know about that," the customer returned.

"It's on its way to being respectable, maybe, now that the railroad's here. But you scratch that dusty surface out there, Finn, and it's still the Wild West."

Or even wilder, Cissy thought. Was Buck aware that word about him now ran rampant? That with every train that pulled into the station or every stranger who rode into town he might be in danger?

"Sheriff should ask this Buck Standish fellow to leave," the proprietor stated.

"Sheriff's away, over to Buford. You know he's got a lot of territory to cover."

By the time the customer left and the proprietor turned his attention to Cissy, her hands shook almost too badly to hold her basket.

Buck must be warned. He'd be at work now. When she left the mercantile, she looked up the street toward the bank but didn't see him out front. Probably on duty inside.

She could scarcely go walking in there and speak to him in front of half the town. But she had to make sure he understood the danger he was in.

No, she lied—she also wanted an excuse to see the man. Because not seeing him hurt like pouring salt in a wound, one that reached all the way to her heart.

The day passed in a blur of changing linen, peeling vegetables, and baking. After supper, which she didn't touch, she made short work of the dishes, then cut a piece of pie and wrapped it in a cloth.

She thought she knew where the livery was. Of course, if Mrs. Culpepper found out she'd gone there, she'd treat Cissy to a tongue-lashing unlike any other.

Respectable women didn't go seeking out men at the places where they slept, not even in the Wild West.

She went the long way, circling down Buckboard Alley to Old Cheyenne Road and approaching the livery from the rear. Her ears caught the sounds of music and laughter from the direction of the Wylder County Social Club, on the other side of the railroad tracks. What if Buck had gone there?

Folks still out enjoying the warm evening turned their heads and looked at her. For sure, this would get back to Mrs. Culpepper. She'd better make it count.

Silence greeted her when she reached the stable. Some of the horses were out in the corral. She stuck her head in the big wooden doors, only to be met with the strong scents of horse and hay.

"Cecilia?" Buck appeared from behind her, and she spun. He wore his pistols but no hat, and the sinking sun lit his black hair with a sheen of red.

At the sight of him, Cissy's terrible agony eased. She seized his sleeve and towed him into the stable. Several of the horses raised their heads and looked at her.

Buck covered her hand with his. "What is it? What's the matter?"

"This your berth?"

"What? No, it's down this way."

"We'd better get out of sight."

His saddlebags and other gear lay tucked inside an empty horse box. His mount must be one of those outside. She balanced the dish of pie on the top of the rail and pulled him inside, clasping his fingers tight.

"Did you hear? Talk's all over town now. Everybody—everybody knows who you are."

For a moment he said nothing, just gazed at her from those black eyes that seemed able to see inside her. Abruptly, he nodded. "I've been denying it, whenever anyone challenges me with the name, but I don't think it will fly."

"It sure didn't take long for it to get all over town."

He gave a bitter smile. "It never does."

"But, but—" Why wasn't he more bothered by this, how did he remain so calm? "You're in peril. Some hot gun could come riding into town at any time to face off against you. He might already be here."

"Yes."

She clenched her fingers harder on his. "So you need to leave. Pack up your things and move on before the worst happens."

He stepped closer. "Is that what you want, Cissy? For me to leave Wylder?"

"No." God, no. "But I don't want you killed, either. Or—or for you to kill someone else. It might be for the best."

"For the best," he repeated. He released her hands and laced his fingers through her hair, a thrilling sensation. Cradling the back of her head, he drew her to him. Their lips met, just as if nothing on earth could prevent it—not Mrs. Culpepper's disapproval, and not the chances of a gunfight. They met as inevitably as drawing air, and a woman couldn't live without air, could she?

All the while Cissy's mind hammered at her: she needed to send him away.

Yet when the kiss ended she had no words except, "Oh, God, Oh, God," repeated fervently.

"Not sure I can leave Wylder, Cissy. Not sure I can ride away and see the last of you." He wrapped his arms around her as if he might draw her inside him. "I've never held on to much, in my life. My home, my family, my conscience all slipped away. I don't want to let go of you."

"I don't want you to." She pressed her cheek to his shoulder. "Neither do I want you to die in the street. I almost think it would be better to part with you than to lose you that way."

He sighed. "I haven't met the man yet who's fast enough to take me down."

"No." She lifted her face and looked at him. "Yet there's always the next gunman."

"And the next after that. Maybe you're right, Cissy. Maybe, if I love you, the best thing I can do is ride on out of here, and spare you that kind of hurt."

If I love you.

"And if I love you," she whispered in return, "the best thing I can do is watch you go."

His lips curled in the ironic smile that suited him so well. "Not sure I have the strength for that, though."

"Me, either."

"Cissy, I have nothing to offer you."

"Except—except your heart."

"Except my heart, and I'm not sure you want that. It's bruised and battered, and blackened, but if you do want it, you know it's yours."

"Oh, Buck." *Oh, Buck.* She hadn't come west looking to win anyone's heart. She sure hadn't come to Wylder thinking to stay. But he was here, and that changed everything.

She suggested, "You could turn respectable."

"I'm trying. You see how it goes."

"There must be some town, some place where no one knows you. I'll come with you—anywhere." She probably shouldn't admit that but, damn it all, she was past saving.

He laughed unsteadily. "I thought Wylder was that place."

"Well—well, when these guns turn up to challenge you, you refuse to face them."

"And have them shoot me down cold? Just to say they ended the career of Buck Standish?"

Cissy froze where she stood. "They wouldn't."

"Some would."

"Where's the glory in that?"

"No glory. Beautiful girl, you're better off without me. You deserve more than that kind of life. I should go, for your sake."

"If you go, Buck Standish, I'm going with you."

"Stubborn sort of woman, aren't you?"

"I told you, I'm trouble. Why do you think Aunt Amelia wanted shed of me? And you said trouble always follows you, so—"

He laughed aloud, his teeth gleaming white in the dim light of the horse box. "What am I going to do with you, Cissy Arkwright?"

Cissy, much to her own shocked delight, could think of several wicked, and wonderful, things.

Chapter Fourteen

Hope, so Cissy decided in the days that followed, was a cruel and deceiving mistress. She consistently raised one's spirits, only to bring them crashing down again. And she had a hundred ways of doing so.

Since those moments in the livery when Buck held her in his arms, she'd been unable to banish the memory of their embrace from her mind. Her heart—as stubborn as she was, no doubt—insisted on wishing it might happen again or, worse, that there might be some kind of future ahead for the two of them. Unsuitable, yes, but she hadn't succeeded in persuading her heart to stop reaching for the unsuitable.

The man was in her blood now, like a sickness—the scent of him, the taste, and the warmth of his hands. She'd never imagined falling so deeply in love. Not Cecilia Arkwright, with a good head on her shoulders. She would never throw it all over for the sake of a man. But who could imagine a man the like of Buck Standish?

She'd had hope, too, of solving the problems that existed back in Chicago, getting an answer from her father's lawyer about the existence of a will. But though the Wednesday stage brought a letter from Mr. Pelican, it wasn't what she wanted to read. Though her father's will had indeed come to light, James Arkwright had named Uncle Benjamin as executor. Her uncle had the right to make decisions about their shared business—and Andy's future.

It frustrated her so much she wanted to stamp her foot and spit. She needed to make some decisions about Andy. What was best for him? Should she bring him here to Wylder, to share what must be an uncertain existence? Or leave him where he was, his advantages in place? If she did decide to bring him west, would her aunt and uncle let him come?

She was willing to fight for him, but she needed to be sure about the benefit of that for which she fought. If she thought she and Buck had a future together—well, that would change things. For, despite his past and reputation, she believed him a good person. If Andy might have the influence of such a man in his life, one who could teach him to be honest and strong, she'd face Uncle Benjamin and any lawyers he decided to range against her.

She'd thought about it all day long while she performed the myriad chores Mrs. Culpepper assigned, and all night while she lay in her narrow bed. She felt like a woman in a tiny boat, tossed on an angry sea. One moment, she had faith she—and possibly Buck—would reach land together. The next, she feared her fate lay at the bottom of the waves.

True, Buck had said nothing about a shared future. Like a brazen hussy—and yes, perhaps she was one after all, just as Aunt Amelia claimed—she'd continued sneaking away to see him in the evenings, after all her chores were done. Mostly, they would sit in the stable box and talk, sometimes with Midnight close by. Sometimes she would give in to overwhelming temptation and reach for him. They would twine together while she absorbed the taste, scent, and warmth of him. Always, always she pushed it a little bit farther—one more kiss, one closer embrace, a hand that traveled where it likely should not. And when she left, she did so grieving for what might never be.

She wanted him. An honest woman at heart, she admitted that to herself. Whether she should have what she wanted proved a dilemma she couldn't easily solve, and the one that kept her sleepless at night. A decent woman would back away from temptation. A hopeful one might keep reaching. Which was she, in the depths of her soul?

She wrote back to Mr. Pelican, asking him to send her a copy of Father's will and inquiring what it would take for her to gain custody of Andy. She also asked him to keep from sharing her private business with Uncle Benjamin and hoped he would respect that request. She tried to imagine a future she and Buck might have together, even while his name continued to circle around Wylder like a bad wind.

On a Monday night, she let herself in through the kitchen door, following a visit with Buck. They'd taken a stroll across the railroad tracks through the dark, accompanied by the music from the Wylder County Social Club which, filtered by distance, had sounded enchanting. They'd spoken of many things and laughed at a few, until Buck reached out and caught her fingers in his. Just as if they'd done it a thousand times, and as inevitably as everything else about their relationship, their fingers interlaced and their palms pressed together. She could feel the calluses on his fingers and the strength surging down his arm. Her whole being strained toward the man he was, and what he meant to her—without question, the most romantic thing she'd ever experienced, or dreamed of experiencing.

They'd stopped walking then. He'd turned her gently to face him, and he'd kissed her. A real kiss, and nothing tentative this time, it told her more clearly than any words he might speak what he thought of her, how he felt for her, and what he wanted for the two of them. The same thing she wanted. If only there was a way…

She'd wound her arms around his neck and held on for her life, as to the hope in her heart that wouldn't quite die. She needed him to be part of her future.

She couldn't imagine a way.

Leaning against him weakly—she, a woman who refused to surrender her strength—she moaned words she should never, never speak. "Buck? Buck, I want us to be together. The way…the way a man and a woman are."

He gasped, and she kissed him again, shameless. For several glorious minutes, she thought her heart had won. But she felt him put the brakes on his impulses, felt the struggle throughout his body, so hard against hers, when he drew away.

"Cissy, we can't."

"Why? Why, Buck—"

"It's not right. And you—by God, you're the kind of woman who deserves better than a quick grope in the dark."

"I'm the kind of woman who knows her mind, and what she needs."

"You'd better go home, Cissy. Now, while I can still send you."

No one ever sent Cecilia Arkwright anywhere. True, she'd been sent to Mrs. Culpepper's by Aunt

Amelia, but she'd only gone along with it in order to keep Andy where he needed to be. Now she wasn't sure what was best for her brother. And she wasn't sure how to keep from throwing herself at this man's feet.

A terrifying, thrilling, and wonderful proposition.

How would it feel, offering herself completely to him, and having him accept? How, in his arms, skin to skin, and spirit to spirit? For she loved this man's spirit as much as anything else about him, the strength that had let him leave home as a boy and survive, the inbred gentleness.

The very same trait that caused him to send her away now.

"Buck." She breathed his name into his mouth as she kissed him one last time. With what dignity she could gather, she caught up her skirts and stared him in the face. What did she see in the midnight black of his eyes? Regret. Desire. The hard discipline that remained as much a part of him as the wicked humor. "I'll see you tomorrow night." She stated it in order to fight against the possibility she wouldn't be with him again, wouldn't touch him. "We'll go walking and—and do all the proper things you think a lady should do."

"Cissy—"

"No, it's all right. I understand. You're a gentleman."

"Me?"

"You just don't know it."

She'd walked home trailed by the sound of piano music from the Social Club, aching. Half a dozen times she wanted to turn back, run into Buck's arms, tell him she cared less for decency than for feeling his hands on her.

A woman didn't do that. Perhaps not even this incorrigible woman.

She'd opened the kitchen door as quietly as she could and stepped in to find Mrs. Culpepper waiting for her, standing beside the kitchen table with her arms crossed on her generous bosom. Mrs. Culpepper's hard, blue eyes gleamed like two marbles.

"Where have you been?"

Cissy's heart sank. "I beg your pardon?"

Mrs. Culpepper pointed at the door. "What were you doing out there?"

"I…went for a walk. It's such a warm night."

"Liar!" The word came roundly, and brought the heat up into Cissy's face, less embarrassment than rage.

Thinking quickly, she said, "It's the truth. I've taken to walking every evening. I'm cooped up in this hot kitchen so much—"

"And where do you go, when you take these evening walks?"

"Just around the town. Trying to catch the air."

Mrs. Culpepper's eyes narrowed like those of a snake. "Amelia tried to warn me about you. I swear, I didn't get a letter from her this last year but she complained about what a willful disgrace you were. I only half believed her. It's hard taking in relations, especially when they're not your own blood. But I have to say, she was right."

Cissy said nothing. Her cheeks flamed.

"Send her to me, I said. I'll straighten the minx out. All that's required is a dose of hard work and good moral restrictions. Not that Amelia isn't a moral woman. But she'd about lost all patience with you. I have to say, though, nothing I've tried has made a lick of difference."

"I beg your pardon? I've done every task you've put before me in this house."

"You have. In your own, stubborn way. You'll wash this floor if I force you to. And you'll work at that stove if I ask, but you're more interested in baking your own fancies than in feeding my boarders. Men need meat and potatoes, not three-layer cakes."

Cissy thought of Buck's face transforming with joy as he bit into one of her desserts. "That's not so. In a world full of hard things, it's essential to have something above the rudimentary, from time to time."

"Above the rudimentary?" Mrs. Culpepper sneered. "There you go again, declaring your own opinions and insisting your ideas are better than mine. May I remind you, you work for me? This is *my* boarding house, and the rules I make are to be obeyed."

Cissy's chin came up. "I will never keep from speaking my opinions. Just so you know."

Rage flared in Mrs. Culpepper's eyes. "You, young woman, have no shame."

"Why should I be ashamed?"

"You were seen. Seen!" Mrs. Culpepper raised up on her toes, rife with indignation. "Meeting a man. Did you really think you could sashay around the streets of this town like a—like an alley cat, and it wouldn't get back to me?"

Dismay mingled with the anger in Cissy's heart, making her go suddenly weak in the knees. Yes, she should have known that. Any woman with a grain of sense would have known. But the need to see Buck, to be with him, and the hope of touching him, had taken her beyond such restrictions.

Damn that tendency to hope, anyway.

"I've done nothing wrong."

Mrs. Culpepper howled. "There, my girl, we have the heart of the problem. You see nothing wrong in a young, unmarried woman slipping out of a house—a respectable house, I might add—till all hours of the night. To see a man. I am responsible for you! I promised Amelia I would put you on the straight and narrow. How am I going to tell her just how far you've fallen? Why, you might just as well go work at that shameful place the Wylder Social Club as stay here and continue working for me."

Cissy struggled to draw a breath. Did Mrs. Culpepper know who she'd been meeting? Because that would just put the frosting on the cake.

"I should toss you right out of here, on your ear. And I tell you, Cecilia, if you weren't the niece of my bosom friend, I would do just that. You have destroyed your reputation—and mine."

"I'm sorry you feel that way, but I'll say again, I've done nothing wrong." Except for meeting the most desirable man she'd ever encountered in the dim reaches of the stable, over and over again. Despite lengthy, delightful conversations during which she tried to think of any possible excuse to move into his arms, where she wanted to be. Despite long, long sweet kisses when her tongue dueled with his in a manner that rendered her damp with longing. She wanted to know where that longing might lead them, how it felt to meld together with Buck Standish, and belong completely to him.

"Well, if you can stand there and say creeping around of the evening isn't wrong, and does not make you a harlot, then I—"

"I am not a harlot! Harlots accept money for what they do—"

Now Mrs. Culpepper's face flamed. "A tramp, then. A she-cat in heat. Do you like that better?"

Cissy didn't. But at the moment, she worried more about Buck than herself. "Who spoke to you about me?" And did the informant know whom she'd met?

"Never you mind. This town has eyes, and a good thing it does. Because your behavior has to stop. How can I send you back to Chicago completely ruined?"

"Do you mean to send me back to Chicago?"

"I haven't yet decided. I intend to write immediately to Amelia, and seek her advice on what should be done with you."

What should be done with her.

Cissy bristled. A grown woman with competent albeit rash tendencies, no one had the right to do anything with her. It was time she stepped out on her own, took her life—and quite possibly Andy's—into her two hands. But what if her reputation here in Wylder had truly been sullied? How could she hope to seek other, better employment or perhaps establish a business—now, there was a wild dream!—if the people with whom she had to deal shared Mrs. Culpepper's opinion?

Mrs. Culpepper added, "I should toss you out tonight."

"I'll pack my things." Where could she go? She had no money for a room elsewhere. No friends in town, yet, upon whose mercy she might toss herself. She certainly couldn't go to Buck. Not only was it utterly unsuitable, but it would draw undue attention to him.

“Don’t be so hasty. I owe it to Amelia to keep you here and safe until a decision can be made. But as a condition of allowing you to stay here, Cecilia, I want the name of the man you’ve been creeping out to see, and I want your complete assurance you will not see him again.”

A breath puffed out through Cissy’s lips. She didn’t know. Mrs. Culpepper absolutely did not know she’d been seeing Buck Standish, notorious gunslinger at large. “Your erstwhile informant did not name him?” she challenged, perhaps unwisely.

“They—for it’s more than one person saw you—did not. Merely saw you sneaking around and walking with some man. Hand-in-hand, so I was told.” Mrs. Culpepper’s tone declared that walking hand-in-hand with a man equaled stripping off all her clothes in the middle of Wylder Street.

“Is it wrong for me to go courting?”

“Not at all, provided you’ve introduced the person in question to your guardian—who at this time happens to be me. I can only think your failure to do just that means you’ve overstepped the bounds of decency.”

“Meaning?”

Mrs. Culpepper’s flush grew hectic. “That you’re sneaking around because you’ve—given away your virtue. Like the cat in heat I described!”

“I haven’t.” Not yet. And not for lack of desire.

“Tell me his name and bring him here to meet me, or break off this ill-advised relationship.”

“Mrs. Culpepper, I’m twenty-four years old. You will not give me ultimatums.”

“I will, if you wish to remain beneath my roof.”

Cissy shook her head. “I refuse to identify him.”

“Then I can only assume the worst. I will write to your aunt immediately. You may stay in your room and continue working here till a decision is made. But if—” Mrs. Culpepper’s eyes narrowed again, viciously, “if you go sneaking out again, I will toss you out in the street.”

“Understood,” Cissy replied with what dignity she could muster. It was all she could speak, for now. But oh, how was she going to get word to Buck?

Chapter Fifteen

"I've been hearing an awful lot of rumors about you."

Buck, standing at the corral and stroking Midnight's nose, turned when livery owner Chet Daniels spoke behind him. He'd just come from his shift at the bank, later than usual because Mr. Mountroy had hired a new man for nights and wanted Buck to show him the ropes. He'd hoped Cissy would be here ahead of him. It had been two nights since he'd seen her, and quite frankly the promise of meeting her here was all that got him through his days.

The first evening she didn't show, he hadn't worried. He figured something had come up at the boarding house. But his disappointment had been considerable. Only when she failed to make her usual walk down to the livery did he realize how much he looked forward to their evenings together. And not just the kisses—he missed her conversation, and the incomparable feeling of comfort he got when she was near.

He'd never known anything close to that feeling.

Now, he was getting worried. Which was what he'd just been telling Midnight.

"People talking about me, eh?" he asked Daniels. No point in trying to deny it. He heard the whispers himself and caught the stares all day long while on duty at the bank. He figured if he had a lick of sense, he'd saddle up this horse and leave. But that would mean never seeing Cecilia Arkwright again. And he could barely go two days without her, God damn it.

"They say you're this well-known gun for hire, Buck Standish. Is that true?" Daniels looked directly at Buck with his honest, brown eyes.

Buck sighed. "Don't want to lie to you, Chet. You've been good to me, letting me stay here with Midnight, now that I've lost my berth at the boarding house. If I said that's why I lost my bed there, and that I was this fellow—Buck Standish—would it make you want to throw me and Midnight out?"

"Well, I don't know." Daniels rubbed his chin. "I like you, Saunders—though it's apparent that ain't your real name. You seem like an honest man."

"I try to be."

"And that ain't at odds, necessarily, with being a hired gun. I've known a variety of fellows who lived by their guns. They were as different from each other as tailors, or blacksmiths. I reckon men are men, no matter what, and need to be judged on their own merit."

"I appreciate that."

"Having said so much, I don't want no trouble here. I can't afford no trouble here. I'm responsible for the care of other men's horseflesh. If somebody comes looking for you, to challenge those guns of yours, bullets will fly. And there's many an innocent bystander—man and horse alike—who's been gunned down by accident."

"I understand." Buck's heart sank. He and Midnight could bed down on the prairie if need be. But if Cissy came looking for him… He glanced for the tenth time down Old Cheyenne Road, the way she usually came. No slender figure with hair brighter than the moonlight. And his disappointment was all out of proportion. She was just a woman, wasn't she?

Wasn't she?

He told Daniels, "If you want us to leave, we'll go."

"Well, now. I might be inclined to let the horse stay. He's a nice enough animal and hasn't caused me any trouble. To be fair, you haven't caused me any trouble either, yet. And like I say, I like the fact that you've been honest with me. Say, if you are this fella everybody's claiming—Buck Standish—mind telling me something? How'd you get into the life of a gunslinger, anyway?"

"I left home young and had to earn my way somehow."

"Yeah, but folks are saying you're one of the fastest that's ever lived. That kind of thing ain't learned, is it? More of an inborn talent."

"I don't know about that." Buck gave a wry smile. "My father came from England where his family owned considerable property. He claims one of his ancestors—part of the landed gentry, he was—engaged in any number of duels and was never defeated. Supposedly killed two men. I guess the apple doesn't fall far from the tree."

Daniels' gaze dropped to Buck's guns. "They're also sayin' you got your initials carved on them pistols. That's how we can tell it's you. If I had a nickel for every time somebody's asked me whether I've got a good look at them, I could shut this place up and live the life of leisure."

“Want to see?” Buck pulled the left-hand pistol with smooth precision. At one time, he’d been left-handed, just one of the things that made him a misfit. Now he’d developed the ability to use both hands with equal skill.

He offered the gun, handle first, to Daniels, who backed off a step and widened his eyes. “Well, I’ll be dogged.” His gaze returned to Buck’s face. “It *is* you.”

“I’ll leave if you want me to, but I’m taking Midnight with me.” He’d have to get a message to Cissy somehow, maybe stop by the house up on the corner of Wylder Street. Because he didn’t think he could leave town without seeing her and giving her an explanation. Unless…

Unless the fact that she hadn’t come to see him the last two nights meant she’d decided he was too much of a complication to allow him in her life. He’d like to think she’d tell him so, if that were the case. But hell, she certainly didn’t owe him anything.

He should take it on the chin, like a man. Never in his life had he gone chasing after a woman. He didn’t want to start now, but Cecilia Arkwright meant something to him, damn it. And it had been years—hell, maybe forever—since he’d felt so close, so comfortable with anyone. He didn’t want to give that up.

Chet Daniels continued to stare at him with his honest, brown eyes. “Listen, Mr. Standish, you can stay for now. But if you could make arrangements to room someplace else soon, I sure would appreciate it.”

“That’s decent of you, Mr. Daniels.” Even a day or two would give him a chance to reach Cissy. Perhaps feel her out on how she truly felt about him.

If she were willing to give him a chance, what

then? He still had nothing to offer a woman like her, and he'd be damned if he'd drag her hither and yon with him while he made their living with his guns. No matter how his heart wanted her with him.

Forever.

****

"Cecilia, might I trust you to run an errand for me?"

Cissy turned from her task, scrubbing the big plank kitchen table, as Mrs. Culpepper entered the room. Since the woman had charged her with having the morals of an alley cat, their relationship had been frosty at best. Mrs. Culpepper kept a close eye on Cissy, checking up on her during the day and even popping into the kitchen once or twice the past two evenings to make sure she hadn't slipped out.

Cissy didn't appreciate the scrutiny and didn't like feeling like a child under a nursemaid's eye. She'd been contemplating ways and means of getting out from under the woman's roof, and trying her best to figure a way of getting a message to Buck, but her mind didn't seem to be working with its usual acumen. She felt distracted, her thoughts straying with disturbing persistence to the tall man with the wicked smile. If she didn't see him soon…

"Cecilia, did you hear me?"

"Yes, Mrs. Culpepper."

"I need you to run an errand for me, but I want you to go straight to the mercantile and back again. No straying, do you understand? I want to hear nothing, later, of you sneaking off to meet—well, whoever it is you have been meeting."

Cissy turned from the table and crossed her arms

on her breast. "Why don't you go yourself?" she suggested as sweetly as she could manage. "That way you won't have to worry where or with whom I am." Stupid, she told herself immediately. If I go down Wylder Street to the mercantile, I might at least catch a glimpse of him out in front of the bank…

Mrs. Culpepper's face turned predictably red. "I would, but my rheumatism is acting up something terrible, and it would be an ordeal for me, waiting in line. I should think you'd have some sympathy for me in my crippled state." She indicated the cane upon which she leaned heavily.

Cissy said nothing.

Mrs. Culpepper's face creased in a scowl. "Amelia was right about you. You have no feeling for anybody except yourself. If I weren't clean out of tea and aching for a cup, I wouldn't ask you to do so much as run a simple errand for me."

Cissy sighed. "Never mind, I'll go. Does Mr. Wylder know which kind of tea you like?"

"He does. Here's a dime. And I'll want my change, mind." She held out the coin.

Cissy laid aside her cloth and untied her apron. Would Mrs. Culpepper time her absence? Would she be able to snatch a few minutes to walk by the bank, maybe grab an opportunity to tell Buck just why she'd been unable to visit him these past few evenings? But eyes would surely be watching her every move. And anything she did would get back to this nasty harridan.

She tucked the coin into her pocket. "I may have a long wait at this time of day."

"Why do you think I'm sending you? I can't stand in line, can I?" Mrs. Culpepper sniffed. "Foolish girl."

"Just so you don't think I've gone off gallivanting." Though, Cissy thought several minutes later, when she stepped out into the hot, dusty street, she would if she could.

Backbone straight, and a defiant bubble in her head, she took the time to call in first at the post office, where she was fortunate enough to find a letter from her father's lawyer waiting for her. Standing in the shade of the post office porch, she tore the missive open and read the spidery handwriting inside with some difficulty.

Well, well…so it appeared Mr. Pelican was on her side after all. He wrote that he'd been checking into Uncle Benjamin's financial and business dealings, following a hunch that matched Cissy's own. He would be forwarding a copy of her father's will to her forthwith, but he encapsulated the contents in a few sentences.

Half of the investment business John Arkwright had left behind belonged to her, Cecilia. The other half would go to Andy when he gained his majority. Meanwhile, yes, Uncle Benjamin was named as Andy's guardian, and the overseer of his quarter of the business. The other quarter belonged to Cissy, and Cissy alone.

A little detail Uncle Benjamin had neglected, ever, to mention to Cissy.

She drew a deep breath, options opening up in her mind. If Mr. Pelican could mastermind a way to give her custody of Andy, she might manage their half of the business from afar, or sell out, if she couldn't stomach the idea of working in conjunction with her uncle. Then she'd have the funds to start a new life—here or somewhere else. She would have a chance at true independence.

The trouble was, her heart no longer felt independent. Hurriedly, she walked back up Buckboard Alley to Wylder Street, where she stole another look down toward the bank, hoping for a glimpse of a slim, black figure. No such luck.

No luck at all.

Chapter Sixteen

Wylder's mercantile bustled with activity as Cissy edged her way in. She'd hoped she might be able to complete her errand here quickly and walk home the long way, past the bank and, maybe, the livery, but now she eyed the line between her and the counter with silent aggravation. Mrs. Culpepper had been wise to send Cissy in her place.

And when Cissy got back, she'd not only be expected to make the tea for Mrs. Culpepper, who sat in the cool parlor with her feet up on an ottoman, but fold all the linens as well as bake a cobbler for supper. Her hand stole to Mr. Pelican's letter, which crinkled in her pocket. She had to figure a way out of the dilemma in which she stood.

She began running the familiar daydream through her mind—how to escape Culpepper's boarding house. There must be a way for an intelligent, resourceful woman to walk her own path in the world. Couldn't she devise a route out of the rat's maze in which she was caught?

Here, in the West, a woman might well choose her own path, if she had sufficient courage and determination. But what about Andy? Would it be fair to take him away from everything he knew and transport him to this place of dust and cattle and men who strutted around wearing firearms?

A customer left the store, and she shuffled forward. She'd never imagined living in a place like Wylder. Yet now that she was here, she could barely imagine returning to Chicago and taking up her old life. Dressing in a fine gown every day, worrying about whether her hair was done up in the latest fashion. Listening to gossip from her friends, and attending formal functions that didn't really interest her… No longer spending her afternoons baking—or scrubbing, or hanging laundry out in the tiny yard—and no longer waiting for the moment her gaze met that of Buck Standish and her day truly began.

A heaviness settled on her chest. She didn't like thinking about a life lived without Buck Standish. She was in trouble here, deep trouble.

Two men came through the doors behind her, edging her toward the person in front of her in line—a matron who gave her a dirty look.

"Sorry," Cissy muttered, and went back to her thoughts.

Could she face returning to Chicago? Just a few short weeks ago, she would have answered that with a resounding yes. Now, though—she had changed. Upon arrival in Wylder, she'd wondered what kind of woman would choose to live here in the West. Now, she knew.

Another customer left the store, and she edged up again.

Despite its wildness—or maybe because of it—this town offered Cissy something she'd never dreamed she needed. Perhaps there was a reason she hadn't fit the narrow mold women back in Chicago society were expected to fill. Had it been destiny that sent her to Wyoming? To Buck Standish? A dangerous line of thinking.

Behind her, the two new arrivals began talking. Their conversation caught her ear.

"Yeah, I was there," one said. "Saw the whole thing. Never thought to see a man draw that fast in my life."

"You suppose there's a bounty on his head?"

Cissy's ears perked up. Whose head?

"Don't know about that. But I do know a man rode into town this very morning looked and smelled like a gunslinger."

"Yeah, they have a look. That Buck Standish—he has it too."

Cissy's spine tingled.

"Probably won't be the last gunslinger we see in Wylder. Word gets out Buck Standish is here, they'll come flocking. And he ain't exactly hard to find, right there at the bank and all."

Cissy stiffened. Oh no, oh no, oh—

Two women left the shop, heads close together and gossiping. Cissy missed the next part of her neighbors' conversation.

"—get a better look at those guns of his. Supposed to have *B* and *S* carved in them. Stands for Buck Standish."

Heat drenched Cissy from head to toe. She stole a look over her shoulder. The two looked like ordinary men, ranchers maybe. Or cowboys. So engrossed were they in their conversation, they didn't notice her eyeing them.

"Something big's bound to happen right here in Wylder—it's just a matter of time. Maybe we'll even get to see it. Not every day you get a chance to witness a fellow of Buck Standish's caliber drawing his pistols."

"Does Sheriff Hanson know? Seems like something he might want to keep an eye on."

A snort greeted the observation. "Sheriff's out of town more than he's here these days. And that deputy of his—"

"Still, somebody maybe ought to drop a word in the sheriff's ear."

"Don't worry. Standish may well take off before any of those gunslingers catch up with him. Men like him—well, they don't stay any place long, do they? What's here in Wylder to hold the attention of Buck Standish?"

What, indeed? Cissy asked herself as she crept forward again. Certainly not the company of a woman from another world—who had a reputation of her own for being difficult. Why would any man consider tying himself to that?

She bit her lip as the shopkeeper signaled her forward. She made her request for Mrs. Culpepper's tea, and swept the men in line behind her with another look as she hurried out.

It didn't matter who they were, really. If what they said was true—if men truly rode into town looking for Buck Standish—the situation had already moved beyond dangerous.

Buck had to be warned, and the sooner the better.

****

She worried about it all that afternoon while she folded the linens and fussed over her cherry cobbler, and while she carried platters in and out of the dining room. With her hands in soapy water, plowing her way through the usual mountain of dishes, she contemplated likelihoods and possibilities.

She had to reach Buck somehow. She had to warn him. Quite likely if she told him folks here in Wylder had actually seen the man come looking for him, he would leave. She didn't want him to go. In fact, if Buck Standish left Wylder, it would tear her heart right out by the roots.

However, she couldn't think of herself. If she didn't warn him and somebody called him out—maybe right there in the middle of Wylder Street—she might have to watch him kill a man.

Or die.

That thought set her hands to shaking so badly she nearly dropped one of Mrs. Culpepper's teacups. No question but she had to tell him. Sacrifices must be made. That was what a woman did when she—

Loved a man.

And oh, yes, she—Cecilia Arkwright—most certainly did love Buck Standish. She'd fallen right down that slippery slope and made the shattering descent into hopeless love. She felt that way—shattered—and as if Buck was the only person who could possibly put her back together again.

And she had to send him away.

Mercy, how would she ever bear it?

And what if it had already happened? If he'd come face to face with some slick gun, hungry for a chance at the big name, and she'd failed to hear? What if—

Oh, she couldn't live like this. But she couldn't live without him, either.

She had to find a way to reach him. To warn him that men who'd come hunting him could be anywhere in town. Before the worst happened, she had to do the one thing she couldn't countenance and send him away.

Would Mrs. Culpepper hear, if she slipped out now? The woman had taken to checking on her nightly, just around the time she finished doing the dishes. That meant soon.

Sure enough, the door to the dining room opened, and Mrs. Culpepper, dressed in her nightgown and slippers, peered in. "Cecilia, my rheumatism is making an absolute martyr of me. I'm off to my bed early." She fixed Cissy with a steely eye. "You're to finish your work here and go straight to your room, hear? I want your promise on that."

"Yes, Mrs. Culpepper." Cissy would do more than lie for Buck's sake. Was he a bad influence? Or had she always been this way, deep down inside?

"If I hear you've been sneaking around the town again behind my back—"

"You certainly won't, Mrs. Culpepper." Not if Cissy could help it.

"Very well then. But you're here on your honor. I want you to remember that."

Honor could be bent, Cissy thought shamelessly as the door closed behind the woman. The heart, on the other hand, just broke.

Hastily, she finished up the last of the dishes and dried her hands. She'd have to slip out and run—run, not walk, and hope nobody saw her. Perhaps a shawl lifted up over her hair would help—her darned hair, as much an identifying feature as if she flew a white flag.

Her thoughts suspended when a knock came at the back door, a very soft knock. If she'd been shut away in her room, she might never have heard it. As it was, she went and hauled the panel open, her old nemesis, hope, rising in her heart.

Could it be—?

He stood there in the dusky gloom of the yard, looking very much the way he had the first time she saw him, when she'd dashed her bucket of dirty water all over him. The expression on his face now, though—in his eyes—was different. Tentative. Inquiring. Hard held, as if he would turn away quickly if he didn't find a welcome.

As if she could ever, ever fail to welcome this man into her heart.

"Buck?" Involuntarily, she glanced over her shoulder. "You shouldn't be here."

"I know I shouldn't. Come outside with me." He touched her. Just reached for her hands, but after being apart only a few days, it was enough to set her to trembling.

"No. We'll be seen." Had he been seen, coming here? She could only hope not. "Come in here, instead." With another desperate glance for the door that led to the dining room, she towed him into her bedroom. Dim and quiet, it was filled with her possessions—a place no man had ever been with her.

She looked up into his face. So tall here in this tiny space, so terribly masculine and potent in a way that fair dazzled her senses. Having him in the very place where she'd entertained such persistent fantasies of him night after night shook her so all the words that had been crowding her head evaporated clean away.

He lifted one of his hands from hers and cupped her cheek. For such a big man, his touch felt wondrously gentle. "Cissy, I've been worried half sick about you. When you didn't come by the livery to see me—well, I know you don't owe me anything. And you have no reason—absolutely none—to want my company or my conversation. But it set me to wondering if you'd thought better about, well, about associating with a man like me."

"No. No, it's not that." Cissy fought the desire to close her eyes and turn her lips into his palm. "Mrs. Culpepper found out I'd been slipping away in the evenings. I was seen out and about, and someone ran to her with the tale. She threatened to toss me out of here if it happened again. I wanted to get word to you, but I just didn't know how."

"Last thing I ever wanted was to make trouble for you."

"It doesn't matter." At this moment, nothing else mattered. "You're here now. And I'm glad, so glad..." But she had to speak a warning, even if it sent him away.

"Buck, did you hear? You're in danger. At least one gunslinger's already here in Wylder, looking for you."

He went very still, and his face, hazy in the dim room, became expressionless. Cissy gazed at him, waiting for a reaction—any reaction—but he said nothing.

"Buck? Did you hear me? I said—"

"How did you learn this?"

"I was in the mercantile. Two fellows—I have no idea who they were—behind me in line were talking. But surely, surely it's all over town—"

"It is. I just didn't want you to find out. Cissy—Cissy, I want to protect you from all this. I need to protect you from this."

"Buck, there's no need to worry about me."

"There's every need."

"I'm not the one who's in danger. One of these men—these gunmen—could come up on you at any moment."

"Hell, Cissy, you think I don't know that?" His hand caressed her cheek. "You think I'm not aware what a perilous existence I live, or that you deserve better? I should walk away from you now." He closed his eyes for an instant. "I just don't know if I can."

She melted. The sensation started where his palm touched her cheek and traveled downward, spreading heat, calling up impossible need. Her heart reached for him, this man whose spirit spoke to hers like no other.

"Buck—"

"I didn't come here tonight to tell you goodbye. I came to make sure you're all right. But it seems—it seems goodbye's what I should say."

"No." She breathed it, barely a word.

"I've been living a dream. But one thing I've learned in life is that dreams end. And for me, it always ends this way. It's like being stalked by a specter, and no matter how I try I can't get it off my tail. I don't know why I thought it would be different this time."

She parted her lips to speak. He didn't give her the chance. The flood gates had opened for this quiet man who usually spoke so little. Words flowed out. "I do believe there's a curse on the men of my line. My grandfather—he should have been a wealthy man back in England. But he had a specter too, one that made him gamble away his ancestral lands. His ancestors shot men dead in duels.

"And my father—his specter was the drink. Whisky made him beat his children and verbally demean his wife. He didn't even try to get his ghost off his tail. I want mine gone, Cissy. More than anything, I want the chance for a future with you."

Tears rushed to Cissy's eyes. She didn't cry often, except in anger or frustration. But now all her defenses crumbled. "There's nothing I'd like more, Buck, than the chance for a future with you."

He laid his forehead against hers. "That means a lot, honey, more than I can say. But it isn't going to happen. Seems if I care for you—if I love you—the best thing I can do is walk away. Saddle up Midnight and ride on out of here tonight." He shuddered on a drawn breath. "And I do love you, Cissy Arkwright."

"I love you too. That's why—if you leave Wylder, Buck, I'm going with you. Just give me a few minutes to pack up—"

"No, Cissy." He closed his hands on her forearms. "No, honey. I can't let you do that."

"You can't tell me no." Almost nobody succeeded in that, and certainly not this man.

"It's no life for you, no life for any woman. Listen to me, sweetheart—my best chance for a new start was here, in Wylder. But the past's caught up with me. It always does, and probably always will. I won't drag you hither and yon, all around the West without a home to call your own."

"But—"

"Listen to me. What about your brother? What about your plans for getting him away from Chicago and out from under your aunt and uncle's influence?"

There was that. She needed a stable place for

Andy. But oh, if Buck left, he would take her heart, and how could she live without her heart?

"You deserve better." Tenderly, he thumbed a tear from her cheek. "So much better. A proper home and a man who can look out for you—"

"You can look out for me."

"Honey, I couldn't even look out for my ma. Or my sister, who married way too young just to get away from our pa. I don't even know where she is now. Does that sound like I can look after you?"

"Together," she insisted, reaching up to cradle his face in turn, "together we can build something good, Buck, something real. You don't have to do it alone. We can look out for each other. I'm strong enough to give you a safe place to be. Take me with you."

"Cissy, girl, I can't."

Panic seized her, raw and bright. "If you ride out of here without me, I'll never see you again."

"You don't know that. Life is long, and full of turns and windings. But I want you to promise me something. You won't wait for me. If you decide to go back to Chicago after all, or you meet some fine man here, someone who deserves you, I want you to grab hold and take the life you deserve."

Maybe Cissy's tears were tears of anger after all. She felt mad enough to hit him. Or to kiss him. "Fool. I don't want any man but you."

"And I don't want you to see me cut down in the street, when the fellow who's faster than me finally shows up. Not that street out there or any other here in the West."

"That would probably kill me," she told him somberly, gazing into his eyes. "But it will kill me just as quick to lose you any other way."

"Don't cry, Cissy. God, don't cry." He drew her closer in his arms. And just like that, Cissy's anger transformed into passion. She wound her arms around his neck as he began kissing her tears away, his lips as gentle as his touch. The sweetness of it had her pressing closer, seeking his mouth with hers.

This—this was where she was meant to be. This moment, this night, and for all time. There must be a way she could show him how much she needed him, how utterly right it was for them to be together.

She showed him with her lips, with her mouth, and with her body pressing hot against his. She told him with the fervor of her kisses, and with her fingers, digging into the silky hair at the nape of his neck. She spoke with her sigh that surrendered all she was to him.

"Tell me you'll give me at least one night, before you go. Buck Standish, say you'll stay this night, here with me."

Chapter Seventeen

In the soft, dim air of the bedroom, Buck could barely see the expression in Cissy's eyes. He didn't have to. He knew they'd be filled with demand, with a hint of challenge, with that sparkling edge of daring he loved so well.

He couldn't let her offer herself to him. No mistake, that was what she intended with her persuasive kisses and her body pressed so close against his. She wanted the same thing he did—for them to be together, the way only a man and woman could be, at least once before he rode away.

One night in her arms. Was it too much to ask? It suddenly seemed he'd asked very little from his life. Escape from the strap his pa liked to wield. Survival, which meant a fast gun. A place to rest a while.

Well, he'd found that place—only it wasn't a place but a woman. And damn it—*damn it*—he would have to give her up.

It made him want to weep, and him a grown man. It made him want to wrap her more tightly in his arms, dive into her, show her exactly how he felt for her, even if that meant he made her his own. Especially if that's what it meant.

"Cissy." He gasped her name, open mouthed. "This isn't a good idea. Not at all."

"Hush."

"But I can't let you—"

"Nobody lets me do anything."

He laughed unsteadily.

"I want you, Buck Standish. Are you going to tell me no?"

"I—"

She kissed him deeply. As a means of shutting him up, it proved powerfully effective, sending a jolt of white-hot lightning straight to his brain, one that burned all his words away. For the span of several heartbeats he knew only sensation—the seductive heat of her mouth, the stroke of her tongue against his. Her fingers dug into the hair at the back of his head, and her breasts—her breasts—

His brain stuttered there. His body took over in demand.

If they took off all their clothes, if they lay on the bed not two steps behind him, maybe then he could show her, show her—

What he could not say. How much he loved her. That he'd be willing to sacrifice anything—anything—to be with her. Even his life.

"Cissy." He broke the kiss and gusted a breath into her ear. "There's no going back from this."

"Shh. Do I have to tell you again? We don't want Mrs. Culpepper to hear."

No, they most certainly did not. Few things would be more horrific than having that woman throw open the door and catch them at what they were about to do.

"Do you think you can be quiet, Buck Standish?"

"Yes, ma'am."

"I want you to know, I believe this is right, Buck. The most wondrously right and proper thing I've ever done." He caught a glitter from her eyes. "I mean to have you at least once before you go riding off. Do you understand?"

He did, and the last of his resistance drained away. No use arguing with a woman this determined. No use at all.

****

Miss Cecilia's skin felt like silk. It quivered under Buck's palm as he slid his hand down the curve of her hip, making his paw seem too big and rough. He was definitely too big for her bed, but she didn't seem to care. She threw her head back on the pillow when he touched her, as if she wanted to savor the sensation, savor him.

She had the most perfect body he'd ever hoped to see, let alone touch. Perfect legs, long and white in the gloom, for they hadn't more than a stitch of light here in her bedroom. Perfect breasts, just the right size to fit in his hands, the nipples peaking atop them in invitation. A man could feast on breasts like that, all night long.

And her hair! She'd taken that down for him last of all, after she slid out of her clothes. After he shed his. She'd rendered him hard—and helpless.

Maybe—maybe he could stay here with her all night. But he had to be careful—to keep quiet, yes, when he wanted to shout. And to stay gentle with her. A man didn't rut with a woman like Cecilia Arkwright. He came to her softly, respectfully, caring more for her pleasure than his own.

Could he bring her pleasure? Him, Buck Standish? The very idea made his head go light.

"Ah." She wound her limbs around him, there in

the bed. Her arms curled possessively around his neck, and her legs encircled his waist. Her breasts nestled in the hair on his chest.

Did she have any inkling what she did to him?

"Cissy." He needed to tell her, declare himself like some damned fool, bare his very soul maybe. But they had to keep quiet, didn't they? What if Eulalia Culpepper heard what she shouldn't and came storming through that door? Holy Jesus, what a scene there'd be then.

"Buck." She spoke his name and claimed him—claimed him for all time.

Had he lived his whole life, up till now, for this moment? Quite likely so. All the pain, all the sorrow, leading to this night in bed with Cissy Arkwright.

A worthy reward.

"Touch me," she whispered. "Show me—not just what men and women do together, but what you and I should."

He bent his head and fastened his lips over the marvelous peak of her breast. The ensuing pleasure completed the process of unhinging his brain. Only disjointed words came. Soft. Warm. Heaven.

She arched into his mouth and gusted the words, "Oh, holy hell!"

He wanted to laugh then—never before had a woman made him laugh in bed—but what they shared felt too significant for laughter. It felt almost sacred.

If his woman wanted to swear or laugh or pray in bed, so be it—just as long as she did it quietly. And with him.

His woman.

So she was, even if only for this one, blessed night.

He transferred his mouth to hers, and she wrapped those long legs around him again, just as if they'd done this a thousand times instead of never. He drove into her, staying as gentle as he could, and she gasped into his mouth. They held onto each other, no longer two separate souls alone in the world but truly—truly one.

One place of belonging, shared by two.

It had been so long since he'd belonged anywhere, it fair stunned him. He buried his face in Cissy's hair, hanging on, hanging on, and tears stung his eyes.

Now this—now she—was worth dying for.

"Buck. Buck," she whispered his name. Another prayer? No laughter in her voice now. No pride. Did she feel as humbled as he?

"Yes, darling girl?"

"I love you."

A lump appeared in his throat, big enough to choke him.

"Buck?"

"Hmm."

"That's why I've decided you're right. Anything's better than seeing you hurt. If that means you need to leave Wylder without me—then you have to go. Now. Before it's light." Defying her words, she wrapped her arms more tightly around him.

Buck distinctly felt his heart come to pieces inside him. Having bonded with her this way, how could he leave her? But she was right. Better that than having her see him gunned down.

She was willing to sacrifice her happiness for him. Could he do any less?

When he failed to answer, she pressed her cheek, wet with tears, against his. "Please. Please."

"Don't cry." He couldn't tolerate tears. Abbigail used to weep when Pa beat him. He hated being responsible for someone else's unhappiness.

"Go now," she begged. "Leave while it's dark."

But the act they'd shared, with its heat and sweetness, had also changed his mind. "Cissy, listen to me. I think I'm just where I need to be."

"If I lose you, Buck, I don't think I could bear it."

"Darlin' girl, you'll lose me either way. If I ride out of here tonight, or if I face some faster gun."

"Yes, but at least I'll know you're out there somewhere, riding that big black horse of yours. Free."

He would never be free—didn't want to be free of the hold she had on his heart. "Free," he repeated. Till he met the next gun, in the next town.

"I could bear that. Maybe." She began kissing him again, weeping all the while.

"Hush," he bade her. "Sleep here with me. When you wake up, I'll be gone."

At least, from her bed and from this room. Nothing—nothing could shift him, now, from Wylder, Wyoming.

Trusting as a child, she curled into him and slept.

Chapter Eighteen

He crept away before dawn, while Cissy still lay sleeping. A mere suggestion of tinted light filled the air beyond the window, just enough to turn her hair, which spread over the pillow, to a blaze of white gold. One sweet breast, still naked, peeked out from beneath the blanket.

She was the most beautiful sight he'd ever beheld.

He wanted to wake her then, ached to say all the words he couldn't. But if he loved her—and he did—he needed to gather up his things and slip out while no one could see him and bring blame to her door.

She didn't wake as he dressed, nor when he scraped open the door of her room and, like a shadow, made his way out of the boarding house. In the murky light that precedes dawn, he stood and tried to catch his breath. Tried to gather his thoughts also, though that was harder. It suddenly seemed to him he'd been running a long time. Away from Pa, and Abbigail's sorrow. All the way through the West, from the Territory of Colorado to California and back again. Now he'd found something worth stopping for. Maybe it was time for him to make a stand.

But how could he do that without harming the woman he loved?

Guns were already here in Wylder, looking for him. This could be the day he got called out. Any day could be. Always before, faced with forewarning, he'd chosen to ride. Now his heart lay in Cissy Arkwright's grasp. He needed to find a way to free himself—if only for her sake.

Sure, he could face whoever came here to town, looking for him. He'd probably win. He always had. But falling in love with Cissy had taught him that there's a first time for everything. And if he got gunned down—for the first and last time—it would break her heart.

A perilous thing, caring more for somebody else's happiness than your own.

He needed to get to work, do his shift at the bank, and then tell Fred Mountroy he wanted out of the guard business. Such work was too close to what he'd been doing so long, relying on the guns at his hips. And then he needed to see if he could turn over a new leaf.

And if he might, just this once, have a fair chance at a future.

****

"Buck Standish!"

The instant the challenge cut through the air—right there on Wylder Street—Buck knew the bad-luck dog that trailed him so long had fair caught up. In the middle of a hot, June afternoon, just when he'd finished his shift at the bank, and his thoughts turned to Cissy once again, the memory of last night's deep and tender loving still alive within him, came the reckoning. But he wasn't ready, he was not ready yet…

He turned slowly to face the man behind him, thinking all the while—he should have known. He should have known he didn't have any real chance at happiness.

His challenger stood posed in the middle of the street, with the late afternoon sun shining full upon him. That light seemed to mark everything out in sharp relief—or maybe it was Buck's senses that sharpened. Did he recognize this fellow? Sometimes men he'd faced before, and failed to finish off, came back looking for a better resolution. A win.

But no. Narrowing his eyes against the glaring light, he ascertained this man was a stranger. Tall and blond-haired, he wore a tan Stetson on the back of his head, and a pair of guns as fancy as Buck's own. His eyes fastened on Buck without blinking, in the kind of stare Buck had seen far, far too often.

Oh, shit. Oh shit, not here. Not now. Not before he got to see Cissy again.

His hands moved on their own, swooping into position and hovering, the fingers twitching in the way they had, that told him he ran on pure instinct. Reflex would save him, if nothing else. The edge of the razor, deadly and keen.

"Buck Standish," the man said again, "I'm Joe Seward, and I'm calling you out."

How many times had Buck heard those words, or similar ones? They usually signaled death—not his, but another man's. Would this be his time it turned out differently?

There could scarcely be a worse place for it. In late afternoon, Wylder Street teemed with people. Women hurried about with shopping baskets, and children played chase. Men went in and out of businesses up and down the street, and horses were tied up all along the way.

Nothing Buck hated more than seeing a horse get

wounded.

"Here and now!" Seward called. All around them, people had begun taking notice, awareness spreading in that way it always did, from the closest at hand, fanning out like ripples in water. Heads turned. Buck heard someone call, "Hey, boys, this is it!"

The man facing Buck grinned a prideful grin. "Right you are! This is the day Joe Seward takes out Buck Standish and earns the title of Fastest Gun."

"Don't be a fool."

Seward sneered. "You scared? I heard Buck Standish never backs down from a challenge."

"That was the old me. Turned over a new leaf."

Seward spat. "Walk away from me, if you're a coward. I'll take you down anyway."

A cry came from the bank. "Get the sheriff. Somebody get the sheriff!"

Seward's sneer widened. "Or you can hand me your guns, big man, and maybe I'll let you live."

He could do that—for Cissy's sake, he could—maybe. On the other hand, he wanted to wipe the smirk off this bastard's face, wanted it so bad it made his fingers twitch harder.

What was he? A man, or just a gun? What did Cissy deserve?

"Too many people around," he told Seward. "Somebody innocent might get hit."

Seward laughed. "Innocent? In this town?"

"It's a good town." Good enough for a man like him. Good enough for a new start.

Folks had begun shifting aside, lining the street, watching keenly. Mothers corralled their children and held them tight. People hung out of doorways.

Everyone—everyone was watching.

And he, Buck Standish, had a reputation to uphold, didn't he?

A vision of Cissy came swimming up before his eyes. White-blonde hair. A rosebud of a mouth, and those eyes that looked at him as if—as if he was the only man in her world. The only one that mattered, anyway.

Did he have the courage to do what needed to be done, for her sake?

"Gunfight! Gunfight!"

The word traveled through the onlookers like wind through corn. As he had innumerable times before, Buck Standish looked into his opponent's face. Here in the dusty street, two lives hung in balance.

No—three lives, for Cissy mattered far more than he or Seward did.

That thought decided him. Even though a throng of onlookers hung on his every move. Even though Mr. Mountroy stood frozen in the doorway of the bank.

Was he a man, or a *man*?

With a snort, he tossed back his head and spread his fingers out in front of him, in a soothing gesture. "You want my guns? That what you've come for? Then take 'em."

He reached for the buckle on his gun belt, and Seward's hands tensed. But Buck was nothing if not quick. Before Seward could blink, Buck's belt—and guns—were off and in the dirt of the street.

It hurt. It hurt, doing that. But it also felt like he shed a weight that had rested on his soul for far too long.

He raised both hands again. "You intend to shoot

an unarmed man in front of dozens of witnesses? I'm done facing fools like you, understand? Done."

Seward glared at him, enraged at being denied his moment of glory. Buck turned his back anyway, and heard that sound—that little, telltale sound—of iron sliding against leather. He started walking away slowly, his head right up, with everybody staring, mouths ajar.

Seward would either shoot him or he wouldn't. Either way, he'd done what he could to put the old life behind him, the only way he knew how.

For Cissy's sake.

He saw her then, rushing straight toward him down Wylder Street, from the direction of the boarding house. Some damned fool must have gone running with the news. She came quick, her white-blonde hair streaming out behind her, almost tripping on her skirts. Her hands reaching—reaching for him.

Behind him, he heard another sound, one he could never mistake—that of a pistol being cocked. He spread his arms wide, making of himself as big a target as possible. He didn't want that bullet going wide and hitting Cissy.

Anything but that.

****

Dust hung in the air, and the sun glared so brightly Cissy had to blink, and blink again. Every surface glittered—the windows of the bank, the harnesses on the horses. The guns of the man standing behind Buck, who'd turned and now came toward her.

But where were Buck's guns? Why didn't she see them at his hips? She struggled to get the hot air into her lungs, running in step with her pounding heart. Only ten steps and she would reach him. Five.

He spread his arms as if to embrace her. She saw something in his face—desperation. Determination. Love.

Oh, my love.

A report came, a terrible, loud booming, snapping sound. Everybody lining the street cried out at once. Still reaching for her, Buck stumbled. His knees buckled, and he went down hard in the street.

Cissy's entire world narrowed with horrifying velocity. She looked at the man who stood facing her, the one who had smoke rising from the gun in his hand.

The monster who'd just shot the man she loved. In the back.

She wanted to run to Buck. Instinct bade her stoop and tend to him, because he lay on his face in the dust, with a red stain spreading across his back. Being Cissy Arkwright—the troublesome young woman Aunt Amelia had banished from Chicago—she rushed past him and flew at his assailant instead, fists flailing and a wail coming from her throat.

"Bastard! You bastard!" she cried before the whole street. "You shot him in the back! You craven, yellow-bellied, cowardly bastard—"

Barreling into him, she took him over backward and kept striking him, blows landing on his cheek, jaw, and chin. After a shocked moment of frozen silence, when Cissy had the maddened satisfaction of feeling her blows connect, a number of the townsfolk, including Fred Mountroy, stepped forward and pulled her off, arms and legs still flailing.

"She's a wildcat, she is," somebody exclaimed. "Did she kill the fellow?"

"No." Someone else bent down. Sheriff Earl

Hanson had appeared as if by magic. “He hit his head when she knocked him down.”

“Let go of me!” Cissy wiggled free of the hands that restrained her and ran back to Buck. Someone else had beat her there—Doc Sullivan, with his bag already in his hand.

Cissy tumbled to her knees. “Is he alive?”

Doc touched Buck with careful hands. “He is, and from what I can see, likely to stay that way.”

“Oh, God! There’s an awful lot of blood.”

“There is, but the bullet’s gone right through. Good thing it didn’t hit the other side.” Doc’s green eyes met Cissy’s, bright in the hot, sunlit street. “Might have hit his heart.”

“No bullet would dare,” Cissy declared. “This man’s heart belongs to me.”

Chapter Nineteen

Mrs. Culpepper turned up not half an hour later and found Cissy sitting at Buck's bedside in Doc Sullivan's back room, Doc having patched and bandaged him.

"He's not going to be happy when he comes to," Doc warned Cissy. But Buck hadn't come to, not yet.

Mrs. Culpepper stormed in like an angry queen bee and lit into Cissy without hesitation. "Get up and away from that man, you shameful girl! I heard what a spectacle you've made of yourself, attacking a stranger in the street."

Cissy looked up and regarded Mrs. Culpepper through narrowed eyes. Did Mrs. Culpepper realize how ridiculous she looked, worrying about propriety when Buck's life hung in the balance?

"I'm going nowhere," she told the landlady.

"You most certainly are. I'm responsible for you while you're here in Wylder—"

"No, you're not." Cissy got to her feet with dignity. "I hereby absolve you of all responsibility for me."

"You're making a show of yourself." Mrs. Culpepper spoke through gritted teeth. "Over a *gunslinger*."

"I guess you didn't see what happened out there. Buck gave up his guns." Somebody had brought them back since, of course, and handed them over respectfully. Doc had laid them on the foot of the cot where Buck could see them when he woke up. That didn't change anything. Buck had—quite literally—walked away from that life, and Cissy knew why.

Mrs. Culpepper swept Buck with a look before planting her nose in the air. "I will need to send your aunt a telegram informing her what's happened, and I'm sure she'll decide this is no place for you. She'll want you back in Chicago at once."

Cissy crossed her arms on her breast. "I'm going nowhere. This is the place for me, here in Wylder, Wyoming. Or anywhere else this man happens to be."

Mrs. Culpepper turned red and muttered, "Shocking!" Swiftly, she whirled and stalked back out, her heels clacking on the wooden plank floor.

Thank goodness.

Cissy, too, swept the man in the cot with a look. Pale beneath his tan, he looked a good deal younger with his eyes closed and his lashes spread in two dark fans against his cheeks. As she watched, they twitched and fluttered. One corner of his mouth quirked.

Cissy knelt down beside him and touched his hand. "Buck?"

His eyes opened, and his gaze met hers—embraced, cradled, and consumed hers. She fell helplessly into a bottomless void, exactly where she wanted to be.

His lips curled farther into the familiar, wry smile. He croaked, "Anywhere this man happens to be?"

"You heard that, did you?"

"Even a dead man couldn't sleep through Mrs. Culpepper's screeching."

His fingers groped for hers, captured them, and squeezed. She flinched; her knuckles hurt from beating on the man who'd shot him. But none of that mattered now.

"You mean what you said?" Buck asked.

"I meant it. Foolish man, I'd follow you anywhere, if you'll have me." Suddenly the tears came, spilled from Cissy's eyes, and fell onto their clasped hands. "What an absolutely rash and reckless thing to do—laying your guns aside the way you did."

"I was laying my old life aside. You deserve better, Cecilia Arkwright."

"I understand what you tried to do. Still—" The tears came faster.

"I guess I'm a reckless sort of man. At least, my heart seems to be pretty reckless. Never would have guessed it, till I saw you for the first time."

"Mine too." She freed her hand, and mopped at her cheeks. She wasn't a woman to snivel or weep, and this wasn't the time. "Still, you should have figured that poor excuse for a man would shoot you—"

"Yep, I figured he might. You were worth taking the chance."

"Oh, Buck! What are we going to do now? We've both burned our bridges." She glanced at the guns on the foot of the bed, with B.S. carved into their handles. "You plan to put those back on?"

"I don't believe so."

"Then, what? You know Mrs. Culpepper's going to chuck me out of the boarding house."

His gaze held hers, and asked a question. "You could live with me."

Cissy nearly gasped as a thrill ran through her, from head to toe. She tried to deny her instinctive agreement as she asked, "Where? In the livery?"

"I reckon we can find another place. You know, the line of work I'm in—was in—" he corrected himself carefully, "paid pretty well. I have some money put aside."

"Oh, yes?"

"I was working for Mr. Mountroy in an effort to turn respectable. But I reckon I have some other ideas."

Cissy mopped at her tears again. "And I've discovered I own a good portion of my father's estate. Once his lawyer, back in Chicago, straightens out that tangle, I will be a woman of means."

"Well, then. I guess it all boils down to taking chances. You're a woman who likes taking chances, right?"

"It seems so."

"Then maybe you'll agree to take a chance on me."

"What are you saying exactly, Buck Standish?"

"I'm trying to ask you to marry me."

Cissy's heart swelled with unbridled happiness. Slipping into their old, teasing ways, though, she tipped her head. "Better do it, then."

"Miss Cecilia Arkwright, would you do me the great and lasting honor of becoming my wife? Before you answer, I feel obligated to point out that as Buck Standish, I still have a reputation. And there might be a spell of time when men continue to come looking for me." He nodded at the pistols. "Till they figure out I no longer wear those."

"You trying to talk me out of this?"

His head jerked on the pillow. "God, no."

Marry him. Live forever in his company. Lie in his arms every night. Share with him the woman she was—no hiding, no pretending—and accept him as the man he was, scars and all. Could she imagine a better fate?

She gazed into his eyes and smiled slowly. “I believe I could consent to staying here with you and taking a walk on the wild side.”

He grinned. “You mean, a walk on the Wylder side.”

She laughed. “Yes, that’s exactly what I mean. But that doesn’t answer the question of where we’ll live, or how we’ll get by.”

“I have a few suggestions about that.”

“I thought you might.”

“I reckon you need to send for young Andy. I know it doesn’t compare with Chicago, but there’s a fine school here in Wylder. And a boy doesn’t learn all he needs to know from a book.”

“I don’t doubt you’re right. You’d welcome him here?”

“If he’s part of you, Cissy, he’s part of me.”

“It will be an adjustment for him. But better than leaving him in Aunt Amelia’s hands.”

“After that, well, Chet Daniels, who runs the livery, has been talking about wanting a partner. I might invest some money there. Just till our other venture gets up and running.”

“Our other venture?”

“Miss Cissy, what’s the one thing this town needs?”

“I can think of a dozen things.”

“How about a bakery? I still say your pie’s the best I ever tasted.”

Enthusiasm rushed through Cissy, right down to her fingertips. What an idea! She wasn’t afraid of hard work, as proved by her stint at Mrs. Culpepper’s. And the thought of being her own boss fair made her dizzy. No one calling the shots except her.

"Run my own business?" she mused.

"With a little help from me."

No one calling the shots except her—and Buck. She could live with that.

Playfully, she drew back and looked at him with mock surprise. "You want to hang up your guns in exchange for an apron?"

He lifted her fingers to his lips. "Not all that much of a walk on the wilder side after all, is it?"

"Oh," she leaned close, "I think it could prove very wild, indeed."

"Then kiss me, Cissy Arkwright. Kiss me and call for the preacher."

A word about the author...

Multi-award-winning author Laura Strickland delights in time traveling to the past and searching out settings for her books, be they Historical Romance, Steampunk, or something in between. Her first Scottish Historical hero, *Devil Black*, battled his way onto the publishing scene in 2013, and the author has never looked back.

Nor has she tapped the limits of her imagination. Venturing beyond Historical and Contemporary Romance, she created a new world with her ground-breaking Buffalo Steampunk Adventure series set in her native city in Western New York.

Married and the parent of one grown daughter, Laura has also been privileged to mother a number of very special rescue dogs and is intensely interested in animal welfare. These days while she's writing, you can always find her latest rescue, Lacy, nearby.

Her love of dogs, and her lifelong interest in Celtic history, magic, and music are all reflected in her writing. Laura's mantra is Lore, Legend, Love, and she wouldn't have it any other way.

Thank you for purchasing
this publication of The Wild Rose Press, Inc.

For questions or more information
contact us at
info@thewildrosepress.com.

The Wild Rose Press, Inc.
www.thewildrosepress.com

www.ingramcontent.com/pod-product-compliance
Lightning Source LLC
Chambersburg PA
CBHW071313200626
46813CB00015B/1854

* 9 7 8 1 5 0 9 2 3 4 2 5 7 *